S0-BDL-420

THE SKY DWELLER

and the Search for Whiloms

Dear Tita Sol,
There's a child in
all of us. It won't hurt to
listen to it's wonderful voice.

AV

♦ Book One ♦

In loving memory of my grandfather, Sixto.

Your spirit and wisdom lives on.

Copyright

Aria Veil's books may be purchased for educational, business, or promotional use. For information, please e-mail
aria.veil.books@gmail.com

Printed and Published by
BOOKS ON DEMAND PHILIPPINES INC.

First printing 2018
ISBN 978-621-8023-52-9

CONTENTS

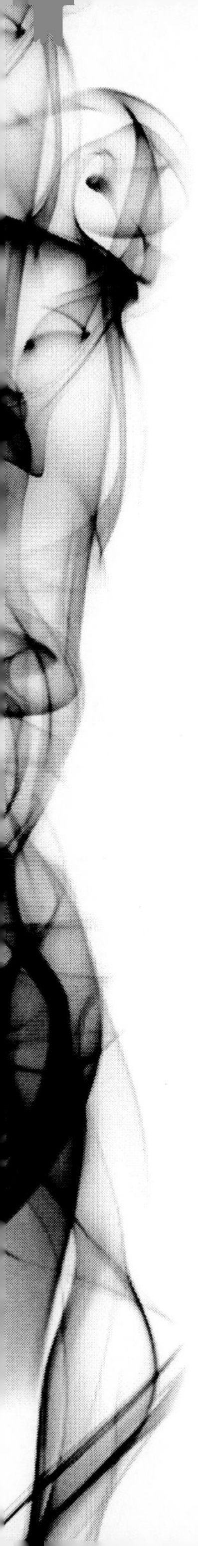

The world
It's filled with noise
Restless
That's how I feel
A voice drowned
In a sea of endless noise

A cut
A rift
A hole
It's there
Silence is there

It beckons to be heard
The silence of one's heart
If you know how to listen to it
Then you might just find the answer

Very few carry that power
A voice so unique and true
That there will be, in that sea –
One original thinker

When all is said and done
You remain
Limitless
Still
Unmoved
Until
The time comes

When you've passed through –
The crashing shallow stream
You find your center,
In the quiet waters of the deep

And there, at the core
Is you
A ripple
A voice
That can silence and break through
All the noise of the world

PART I:
THINGS TO COME

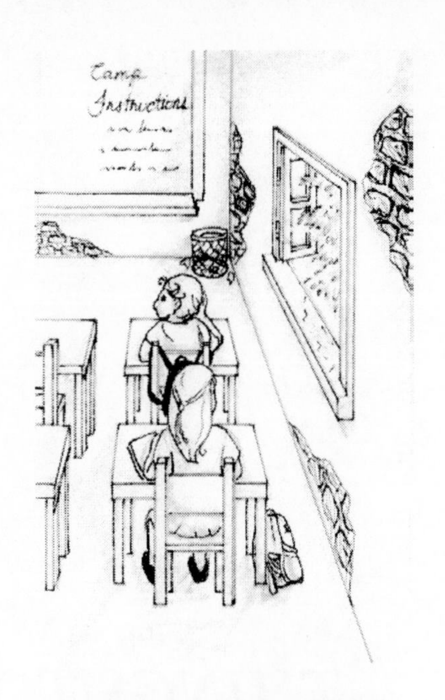

CHAPTER ONE

- Elle -

There was a faint hiss coming from outside. Elle listened closely to the tapping sound the tree branches made as they hit the windowpane.

Tap. Tap. Tap.

"Yo! Elle," Paige said. "I'm so psyched about camp. It's going to be one epic field trip!"

Tap. Tap. Tap.

"What?" Elle replied without taking her eyes off the tree.

"Oh man! Is it just me or does it reek in here?" Paige said. "I think it's coming from Tom's backpack."

Tap. Tap. Tap.

It lingered. The hissing sound was still there. Elle's fingers hurt from squeezing her pencil tight.

"I should just close the window. It might be coming from outside."

She was about to clasp the handles when she noticed a red smudge on the windowsill. *It's blood…or maybe it's—*

Paige shrieked in horror. "What's wrong with him?"

Elle turned abruptly and dashed forward between her classmates. She saw Tom on the floor—his body convulsing.

"I'm going to call for help," Paige said as she ran out of the room.

Where's their teacher? Should they carry him to the clinic? Elle found it hard to just stand there and watch someone having a seizure. Tom's eyes rolled back and his mouth started to froth. Elle leaned in and was about to help lift him up but right in front of her, his face and skin started to change. Everything normal about the boy was gradually turning into something scary—rough scaled skin, sinister red eyes, flaring nostrils, sharp yellowish teeth, and a huge jaw. Elle couldn't believe what she was seeing. He—*it* leaped on top of a desk and started to attack. It was lashing its claws and snapping its teeth, making her classmates scramble out the door. Elle wanted to flee—but couldn't. All she could do was watch and feel trapped in a body that didn't feel like hers.

The creature went down on all fours and the ground trembled as it came and loomed over her. Elle wanted to call for help but it was impossible. She couldn't move—couldn't even close her eyes. The monster was so close she could feel its hot breath prickling her skin. Elle watched, frozen, as it opened its jaw and slowly dug its teeth deep into her flesh.

Tap. Tap. Tap. *Hiss.*

Elle fell out of bed, screaming her lungs out. Her chest was thumping and cold sweat dripped down her forehead. *Okay Elle, you better snap out of this loop. It's just a dream. They are NOT real. There's nothing to be afraid of. Nothing.* Why did she have to dream about those horrendous creatures? Her night terrors were getting increasingly frequent and way more intense. Elle couldn't shake off the feeling of being attacked. It felt so real, and there was that mysterious sound that she heard. That hiss. Could her dreams mean anything?

Elle reminded herself that she should tell Paige about her dream as she grabbed a thick journal from her bedside table and pressed it against her chest. Holding it close comforted her—like a security blanket that protected her against her nightmares. She had only planned on browsing Grandpa's journal and knew that it should be back on his desk come daybreak. Still, she couldn't seem to part ways with it. Elle thought of herself as some sort of detective who just wanted to know more about her departed grandmother. She was that missing apple in their family tree. Why did her family refuse to talk about her? How come there wasn't a single picture of grandma in the family album?

Elle flipped through the first few pages of the journal. She wasn't able to get any lead because the journal was impossible to read. Grandpa was a clever old man. He had written on it using a different language. The only thing readable was the phrase *Find the Whiloms* scribbled on the first page. What were these *whiloms* exactly? And why was her grandfather looking for them?

As she continued to flip the pages, she noticed that one of them was thicker than the rest. It was a folded page. Strange, she thought that she hadn't noticed that before. Curious, she unfolded it. In front of her was a sketch of the monster that had been plaguing her dreams.

"What the—!" Elle muttered as her skin prickled with

goosebumps.

Elle quickly folded the page back and slammed the journal shut. *How is that possible? I should ask Grandpa about this, but who am I kidding? I'm not even supposed to be snooping into the journal in the first place. I might just get reprimanded and never get a real answer.*

Elle got up and walked across the room passing by the vanity. She paused when she saw herself in the mirror. Her forehead was reddish from falling off the bed and her eyes looked tired and had dark rims underneath. She was one-hundred percent sure that her mom would scold her and say things like, *you really don't know how to take care of your skin. Now put some ice cubes* or *cucumber slices on that.* She shook her head. Cucumber slices never really stayed on her eyes for long. They always seemed to slip off. She didn't give much thought about how she looked anyway—a far cry compared to her mother, Emilia, who always had to be glamorous, even as a retired superstar.

Yesterday, her mom had bought a box of brown-colored hair dye because she wanted to hide the most obvious eyesore in their family. Emilia never did like the fact that Elle was the only fourteen-year-old girl in Hillworth that had an odd bunch of silver hair on top of her head. Elle wrinkled her nose. *Nope. I'm not going to have it colored.* In fact, it could even represent her spirit age. Maybe she was an old soul.

Elle pulled off the knitted cap and had to wince at the sight of the unicorn-designed coat stand that her mom had picked out for her. She wore the cap and took a quick glance at the pink wallpaper with dizzying twirly patterns, a plush asthma-inducing carpet, and a chandelier that hung so low from the ceiling that she'd frequently bump her head on it. Elle sighed. She just felt like she had to get away from all this pink.

Elle titled her head as she passed by the chandelier and hopped out of her room through the open window. She half-expected to see blood on the windowsill, but there was none.

She quietly slipped out and grabbed hold of the water tank ladder in front of her. It felt cold under her touch. Once both her hands and feet were firmly onto the steel ladder, she stealthily climbed to the rooftop. Her adrenaline was pumping as she walked over and sat comfortably along the gabled edge of their house.

Elle closed her eyes and took a deep breath. She loved how the wind felt against her skin. The first few times she came up here, she would raise her arms outward and imagine that she was flying. The rooftop was her spot—it was the one place where she could hear herself think and divert her attention from those monsters.

Elle hummed a song that she and her grandpa liked as she looked up at the clear night sky. It was a good thing that their chateau was in the Eastern Sierra, far away from the city's light pollution. From here, she could see the stars clearly. Her lips curved into a small smile. The Milky Way often reminded her of how infinitesimally small she was and the universe was so much bigger. Bigger than herself and her nightmares.

Elle pulled her cap closer to cover her ears. For some reason, tonight felt different. There was something in the air. Just then, she saw a pair of headlights slowly approach—its rays slicing through the stillness of the desert night. When the car stopped in front of their house, its headlights dimmed. From the car, three men appeared.

Elle immediately recognized her grandfather but had to squint to get a better look at the other two. Both men removed their hats as they walked toward the front door. She recognized the younger one—it was the green-eyed boy from her school, Mike. People didn't know much about him except that he was quiet and smart. He was also quite handsome, Elle noted. Back in school, no one had the guts to even ask why he, the headmaster's son, would transfer to Hillworth High so late. It was only last year when he entered the halls of their school.

Elle shifted her gaze to the other man. It was Ben Gabriel, Mike's father and the school's headmaster. Most of the students called him *Big Ben* because he looked as tall as a giant. An exaggeration, of course, but the headmaster really towered over almost everyone in school. Big Ben actually reminded Elle of the wooden owl figurine on the balustrade that led to the front porch. His owl-like features were uncanny. He had feathery gray hair and thick round eyeglasses that made his eyes look bigger than normal. His facial features were rather pointy and calculated.

Big Ben and her grandpa talked as they sat on wooden benches on the porch. Elle listened and was leaning out from the edge of the rooftop, wondering what they could possibly be talking about.

"I don't even know how I'm going to tell her," she heard her grandfather say. "I wanted her outside the gates so she could experience growing up without the burden of it all."

Big Ben made a sound much like an agreement. "My boy will do his best to help. As for me, I feel that my time is near."

She couldn't see them, but she could still see Mike. He didn't seem to be paying attention to their conversation and was peering at the woods that embraced the house.

"Same," her grandfather said. "We will not go silently my friend. However—"

Mike spotted Elle. He was grinning.

Elle scrambled to her feet, but she moved too quickly and lost her footing.

Time seemed to slow down. Elle watched her foot slip, making her lose her balance. She tried to hold onto something—anything that would steady her—but there was nothing but air. There was nothing else she could do but close her eyes, brace for the fall, and hope she wouldn't break too many bones.

Elle waited to feel the cobblestones on her back, but she didn't. She opened her eyes and saw that she was in Mike's arms.

"You alright?" he asked.

Her face burned red with embarrassment, "Yes. I'm very sorry. I know I shouldn't have been on the roof."

Mike lowered her down gently.

Elle got to her feet and tried to straighten out her shirt and calm her breathing. "Good evening, grandpa, Headmaster Ben."

Elle felt flushed. She sneaked a peak at her grandfather. Her eyes widened when she saw him clutching his chest, his face contorted in pain.

"Grandpa, are you okay?" she asked.

"I'm fine, dear," he replied. He tried to sit on the bench behind him, but his knees gave way.

"Grandpa!" Elle cried out, rushing to catch her grandfather, but Big Ben got to him first and helped him sit down.

"No, you're not. You're having a heart attack," he said. "Mike."

Mike quickly stepped forward and put her grandfather's arm on his shoulder. Elle's heart clenched as she watched Mike take him to the car. She could hear him groaning in pain. She should go with him. She had to.

"Elle, listen," Big Ben said. His voice seemed so distant. "Uriel, look at me, dear." This time, he stressed her first name. "Go and tell your parents. We'll meet them at the hospital."

Elle's eyes were still on her grandpa as she nodded to him. *This is all my fault.*

As Big Ben turned and rushed to the car, she dashed to her parent's bedroom and knocked urgently on their door.

CHAPTER TWO

- Mike -

Mike lifted the old man from the car seat and rushed him through the hospital doors. The moment he stepped into the emergency room, he felt a kind of tension electrifying the air—that at any given second, someone nearby could be taking his or her last breath. Mike couldn't help but think of Elle when he lowered her dear grandpa onto a wheelchair. Immediately, a nurse took over the handle and rushed him away.

"Maybe we should have taken him through the gates instead," Mike muttered under his breath.

"No," Big Ben replied. "She can't heal something like this. They only work on inflicted wounds or broken bones or poison. Anything that occurs naturally or is self-induced is going to be a long shot."

Big Ben gave him a stern look. "We shouldn't be talking about this here," his father said. "I got this Mike. I'll wait for Emilia and Leonard to get here. You better head home and prepare everything we need. Have Amos and Erin join you on the mission."

§

The lobby of the mansion housed a wide array of artifacts. There were some armor with intricate details, weapons and scrolls on top of marble pedestals.

Amos and Erin stood by a round table covered with blueprints. They were in the middle of a heated discussion when Mike came in.

"Seriously? What are you guys bickering about at a time like this?"

"Amos almost got discovered today," Erin chided as she pointed her marker pen toward his direction. "Why do I even make these elaborate plans when he's going to mess them up anyway?"

"Then make your plans simpler next time," Amos replied. "Stop making impossible missions that are doomed to fail."

Mike thought of how he'd been fending off bouts between the two. He knew that even though Erin was secretly fond of Amos' quirks, he still was too scruffy for her refined ways.

"How about I make our *strat* this time?" Mike suggested, taking the marker from Erin. "The Pillars aren't going to hold up much longer. One of them just had a heart attack. So, starting today, we double our efforts. What scares me the most is that Elle has no clue about what's really going on."

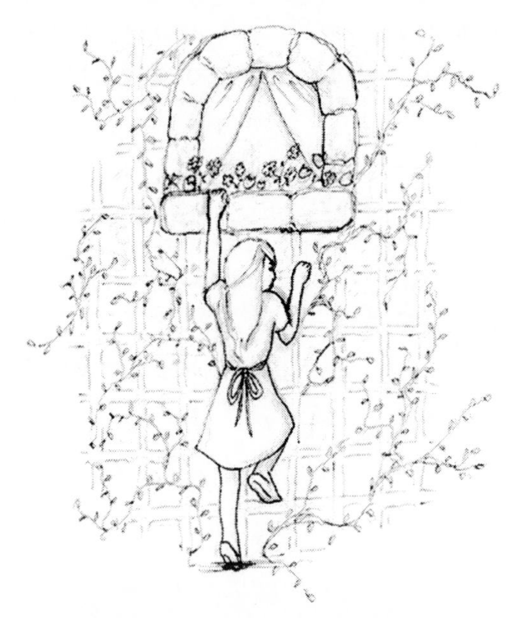

CHAPTER THREE

- Elle -

Elle had already watered Grandpa's garden that morning and was just waiting for her dad to come pick her up.

She had been talking with Paige on the phone as she slid a book into her backpack. In it she saw the journal she had taken. She knew she had to give it back, but instead of returning it, she held it tightly then tucked it back inside her bag.

"Look Paige," she said, "I might not be able to join camp tomorrow. If grandpa stays in then it's a *No Go*."

"Well, that sucks," Paige said on the other end.

"There's always next year," replied Elle, "though it would have been nice to see that 5,000 year-old tree."

"You're such a dork! But I guess that's why we're friends in the first place—we think differently. Look, Silver," Paige said, pertaining to the color of Elle's hair. "Sulking doesn't look good on you. Get some sleep. I know those freakish nightmares bother you, but those eye bags are so goth. FYI, I'm the only one allowed to be edgy here."

"Yeah, yeah," Elle sighed.

Elle heard the front door open. It was her parents.

"Oh, I have to go now, they're here. Thanks for being there for me, Paige. It means a lot. Bye." Elle placed the phone down and carried her backpack.

"Hey, Cupcake. Are you all set?" her dad called out.

"Yeah. I'm ready."

§

The hospital room was small and glum. Almost everything was white—the walls, the bed, and the staff uniform.

Her dad, Leonard, had the TV on and was flipping through the limited channels.

Elle sat on the side of Grandpa's bed, glad that he was okay.

"What book do you have there?" he asked as he ruffled her hair.

"Try to guess," she replied. "*There can be no true goodness, nor true love, without the utmost clear-sightedness.*"

Her grandfather gave an amused chuckle. Elle couldn't help but notice that he had his hand was over his chest—that it took quite an effort for him to laugh.

"In the words of Albert Camus, why yes indeed." He grabbed the book and flipped the pages, regarding it like an old friend. "Elle, we need to talk."

Elle started to worry. *Was he going to tell her about his condition? Is he getting worse? Is he going to... no I shouldn't be thinking about these things.*

"Let's start with a little secret," Grandpa said.

"A secret?" she asked.

"Yes. A secret about the characters in your books."

Elle eased up a little and smiled, "What about them?"

"Well," her grandpa said, "have you ever wondered about what is it that makes them the great *movers* and *shakers* of the world? How are they visionaries? How were they able to find their truest selves?"

"Their truest selves? Or their best selves?" Elle asked.

"It could be both, yes, but in the first place—why is it that most of us get so worked up about how others see us and how we see ourselves?"

Grandpa's words had piqued her curiosity that it made her wonder what the big idea was, "Yeah, most people are like that."

"You know," her grandpa said, "what defines a person's character goes beyond how others see you, or how you see yourself. What matters more, is how you see the world."

"How *I* see the world?"

"Is the world beautiful? Ugly? Is it worth your time? Is it a place full of opportunity or always half-empty? Is the world worth fighting for? Or is it worth destroying?"

"I think I'm starting to understand now," Elle replied.

"These visionaries could see the world from their soul and that enables them to go above and beyond. They try to change 'what is' to 'what could be'. It becomes larger than life. Imagine yourself reaching that point wherein all the petty things that you used to be afraid of won't mean as much to you as the idea you hold in your heart," he said as he pointed to her heart. "That, Elle, is how heroes make something grand with something so small."

Elle lowered her eyes, trying to absorb and remember what her grandpa had just said.

She embraced him gently.

After breaking away, her grandpa's eyes grew as he remembered something, "Would you open that drawer for me dear?" he said while pointing to the bedside table.

Elle did as she was told. Inside the drawer lay a fruit-shaped pocket flashlight keychain.

"Just a little something to light your way," he said.

Elle held the gift tightly, "Thank you, Grandpa," she said as she tried to hold back her tears.

He was about to say something when a knock from the door diverted their attention. It was the food service assistant, bringing in Grandpa's lunch tray.

Elle retreated onto a chair. She pulled out a drawing book from her bag and started to make a sketch of her grandpa. She liked drawing because it helped clear her head. This time, however, she worked harder on making sure that she would remember the details of his face even with her eyes closed.

Elle's dad had been watching an intense football game on the small TV screen when the doctor came, bearing good news.

§

Elle and Leonard were able to bring Grandpa home—back to his cozy bedroom.

Elle was standing by the doorway when her eyes instantly landed on the far left. She swallowed nervously as she saw the small desk where the journal should have been.

Her gaze continued to wander behind the desk where there were old bookshelves that bore rare titles. Scattered here and there were a multitude of air plants inside terrariums. To her right, Elle watched as her dad helped Grandpa lie down on his bed.

"Get some rest, old man," Leonard said with a smile.

Her grandpa smiled back as he endearingly tapped Leonard's cheek.

"Goodnight. I'll check up on you later," her dad said before leaving the room. Elle was about to turn around and leave, too, when she thought of asking something.

"Grandpa," she murmured.

"Yes, dear? Have you been having nightmares again?"

"I always have nightmares," she said. "I just wanted to ask what grandma was like."

Her grandpa squinted and peered outside of the window. "Simply the most beautiful person I've ever laid eyes on. It's not every day that you get to fight for the one you love."

"You fought for her?"

"Yes, and I still do. 'One who has loved truly can never lose entirely.'"

"Hey, I know that line," Elle smiled. "Grandma sounds lovely. Sorry I had to pry. And I'm very sorry about last night. I shouldn't have climbed up the roof. I didn't mean to give you a fright."

Grandpa shook his head. "It's fine, dear. Just, please, be more careful. Besides," he lowered his voice to make sure no one else could hear. "I have a pretty good idea why you enjoy it up there."

Elle snickered. "Grandpa. You're the coolest. Well, I should probably let you get some rest. I'll water the plants first thing tomorrow before heading out to camp so you won't have to worry about it."

Elle thought about the life her grandfather has led as she walked back to her room. The moment she reached her bed, she took out her sketchbook. Elle stared at the drawing of her grandpa and peered into his eyes. *How does one see the world? How does one become their truest self? Will our view of the world really help us find our truest selves? Or maybe it's a matter of helping us narrow down certain choices that needed to be made?*

"My truest self," Elle mouthed to herself. *Now that's something I need to find out. And when I do, I will be able to overcome my fears and fight the monsters.*

Elle had no plans on sleeping that night. She rubbed her shoulder as if she could still feel the teeth that had pierced her skin. Instead of going to bed, she opened her closet and prepared the stuff she needed for camp.

§

Elle was sitting quietly on the bus, but deep inside she was still worried about her grandpa. Beside her, Paige had fallen asleep peacefully. Her best friend always went for the unique and striking look—frizzled hair, mismatched earrings, and green plastic shades that matched her green lipstick.

Elle grinned, remembering how she became friends with Paige two years ago at the school cafeteria. She had been sitting by herself, a girl whose hair seemed to change in color right before her eyes. "Your hair is purple," Elle blurted from across the table.

"No, it's violet," Paige countered. "And your hair is silver. In case you haven't checked the mirror lately."

Elle stifled a giggle and decided to pick up her tray and sat with her. "I'm Elle."

"Yeah, Silver, I know who you are. I'm Paige, and I don't like people sitting with me during lunch."

"How come? Oh, do you want some?" she said, proudly offering her salad. "My grandpa made it."

"Yeah, he made it alright," she retorted. "Like it's so hard to prepare salad."

"Well he did plant them—the lettuce, tomatoes, cucumber, and carrots," Elle said. "He watered it and cared for it 'til it was ready."

Paige stared at her—actually looked at her for the first time. In Elle's mind, she was either being measured, or she had disarmed Paige. The latter was more likely to be true because Paige didn't seem to have a witty comeback or knew that she didn't need one. After all, Elle wasn't really trying to be a smart ass or anything like it.

For whatever reason, Paige started to open up to her. From that day on, Elle noticed how Paige started to mellow down whenever they were together. For one, she stopped trying so hard to be this cool, edgy girl. Paige also opened up to her when she discovered that she was adopted. Paige and Elle may have seemed like polar opposites, but in reality, they were like scales that balanced each other. Paige actually respected Elle's "two cents" on things and often, she helped coax Elle out of her shell, having her speak up if she had something on her mind. She'd tell her that no one was going to condemn her if she weren't perfect, that she didn't always have to say the right things at the right time.

§

The bus ride started to get bumpy. Elle flipped through her grandfather's journal as it lay on top of her lap. She wondered if there was something else she might have missed.

It took her a while to notice that the camp instructor, Ms. Wichpot, was peering down on the journal, too. Elle quickly snapped it shut and stowed it away in her bag.

"What's your name?" the instructor asked in a screechy voice.

"Umm, I'm Elle," she said.

"By any chance," asked Ms. Wichpot as she cocked her head to the side, "is the name of your grandfather, Adam?"

"Yes," she replied. "But only our family calls him that. Do you know him?"

"Oh, more than you know," Ms. Wichpot said with a grin. "Well, buckle up, Elle. It's a bumpy ride."

Several minutes later, Elle stepped off the bus and looked at the scenery. The flowers bloomed with morning dew and the pleasant scent of pine trees lingered in the breeze. From afar, the terrain appeared to have evil-shaped peaks—craggy, misty, and desolate—but now that it was up close, she could see that it wasn't all that bad.

"Dibs on your hands massaging my back," Paige mumbled behind her, stretching out her limbs. "Ugh! My neck hurts, and my butt has cramps."

Elle tried to fight back a snicker upon seeing her friend's sleepy face. "Come on, slowpoke," she said as she pushed Paige uphill towards the Main Hall.

The girls giggled as they raced past the others. They were the first ones to reach the Main Hall. It was a huge cabin. The ceiling had thick beams and a couple of chandeliers. There were rows of tables and different-colored chairs for the students, and at the far end, was a large stage.

As they took their seats, Elle noticed the same camp instructor giving Paige a scrutinizing glare.

"Don't mind it, Elle," whispered Paige. "They will always think of me as a *teenage dirt-bag baby*… and I love it!"

They both laughed.

"I was totally wrong about the grumpy cafeteria lady being your long-lost mom," Elle joked. "I see a big resemblance with this one. *The Force is strong*." Elle couldn't contain herself as they both cracked into a laughing spree.

Everyone settled down as they saw Ms. Wichpot approach the microphone on stage.

"Hi! I'm Ms. Sally Wichpot," she said, her high-pitched voice echoing across the hall.

Ms. Wichpot started to give them a rundown of their two-day itinerary.

"Today, we will get to know each other better. There will be a few talks and then a small gathering tonight at the hall. Tomorrow, we'll have workshops and, of course, bonfire night."

Then, Ms. Wichpot cleared her throat. "Now let's welcome our school headmaster, Mr. Ben Gabriel."

On stage, Big Ben talked with great precision as he reminded everyone to conduct themselves according to the rules of their school. The huge man was just as owl-like and composed as he was when he came over to their house the day before. Big Ben clasped his hands in front of him and looked at the students.

"You are NOT ALLOWED to veer outside the perimeters of the campsite. We may be far away from our classrooms, but that doesn't mean that you may do as you please," he said before handing the microphone back to Ms. Wichpot.

"Alrighty then!" she squeaked loudly. "We'll be grouping everyone according to the color of the chair they're sitting on."

Elle and Paige checked theirs. They were both sitting on blue ones, which deserved a fist bump.

"Uh-oh," Paige said as she looked around. "I think little Miss Pretty is going to be cabin-mates with us."

"Who?" asked Elle.

"The student council president," Paige replied. "She's coming over to us."

Elle watched as the elf-like girl with perfect posture walked demurely towards them.

"Hi, I'm Erin," she said. "You're on the blue team too, so that means we'll be cabinmates."

Elle blinked and saw Paige roll her eyes. "Hi Erin. My name's Elle, and this is Paige."

"Now everyone, listen up," called Ms. Wichpot. "Quickly retrieve your bags from the bus, and then head to the assigned cabin that has the flag that carries your team color tacked on the door. Everyone is expected to return to the hall in forty-five minutes."

While everyone filed out of the Main Hall, Paige gave Elle one of her signature smirks.

"No, Paige," Elle said. "I know that look. You know I always stop your devious plans before they even start."

The moment they left the Main Hall, Paige started to run in a different direction from their cabin.

"Seriously?" Elle mouthed as she ran after her.

"You sure run like a duck," she said when she caught up with her. "Where do you think you're going?"

Paige grinned. "Very funny. I thought you said you wanted to see the oldest tree in world? Don't tell me you don't want to anymore?"

"We should really get back with the others," Elle insisted. "Can we try not to get in trouble on the first day of camp? Big Ben just said we shouldn't be wandering off."

"Don't worry, Silver. I promise, we'll make it back in time. We just need to get there fast, okay? So stop whining and shush."

"I'm serious, Paige."

"So am I. Oh, would you look at that? We're already here."

Elle turned her attention to what Paige was looking at.

Right before their eyes was a Great Basin Bristlecone Pine. It was huge. The trunk and branches twisted in weird angles, and it had greyish-white bark with deep fissures.

Elle breathed in deep as she slowly walked closer. "I was so small when my grandpa brought me here for the first time." She was in awe as she stood in front of the oldest living thing in the world. She touched its bark and felt a certain kind of warmth flow through her. For some reason, she felt a connection to it.

"Ehem!" said a familiar screechy voice. "You two aren't supposed to be here."

Elle turned around and saw Ms. Wichpot near the clearing.

"Oh. Hey! Ummm… What's up?" Paige said, trying to sound cool.

"You two are in trouble, that's what's up," Ms. Wichpot said.

Elle was dumbfounded. This was her first offense.

Paige gave her a smirk and shrugged. "Detention it is."

§

Elle and Paige found themselves sitting on tree stumps outside the Headmaster's office.

Ms. Wichpot came out the door with a satisfied smile. "He'll speak with you one at a time. Elle, you go in first."

Elle stood up and entered the headmaster's office. The room smelled of moth balls, dusty old books, and oak wood. Before Ms. Wichpot closed the door, Elle heard her instruct Paige to head to the Main Hall.

Elle approached the desk. "It was my fault. I wanted to see the tree. Paige didn't have anything to do with it."

The man behind the worn-out desk turned around and smiled upon seeing Elle.

"Oh. I'm sorry," she said, her eyes wide in surprised. "I thought you were Headmaster Ben."

In front of her was a tall man with long white hair and clothes that looked like they belonged in a different century. His navy blue long tailcoat had gold buttons that stuck out like a sore thumb inside the rustic mountain cabin.

"No, Uriel," the peculiar man said in a way that made Elle feel increasingly uncomfortable. "I'm not the Headmaster, but I happen to be something much greater than that. You might call me the Grandmaster of it all."

Elle blinked. She didn't know how to react to such a declaration.

The stranger walked over to a corner where a chess table stood, revealing what appeared to be an unfinished game.

"Ah, let's see. It seems like the pawn here is about to be promoted to a queen." He plucked the pawn off the board and slipped it into the inner pocket of his coat. "We'll see about that. Oh, this is going to be fun!"

Elle looked puzzled, "Well, Paige plays chess better than me. I have to say, I'm a little lost right now."

The man who called himself the *Grandmaster* raised his hand and gestured for her to come closer. Elle's blood ran cold as she watched her legs move on their own. Her legs and feet walked forward—right, left, right, left—bringing her closer to the stranger. She willed them to stop, but her limbs wouldn't obey her. A wicked smile spread on the stranger's face as she came closer. Everything was happening so fast. Was she being hypnotized? Could she be having hallucinations? Her heart started pounding wildly inside her chest.

"My servant was right," he said. "Wichpot knew you wouldn't be able to refuse it. You just had to see that tree."

She was so close to the him that when she peered into his eyes, she saw her reflection in its eerie depths. There was something wrong with his eyes. She looked closer. Her reflection—it was upside down! She trembled, taken aback by how utterly disturbing they were.

Suddenly, something went amiss. The man's expression changed the moment his eyes shot past Elle. His eyebrows were now furrowed in anger.

A window behind her had shattered. Elle couldn't turn her head, but she felt an arm grab her from behind and quickly drag her out of the window.

She saw the Grandmaster pull something out from his coat and speak an unfamiliar language that she somehow understood. He ordered her to bite the arm that was wrapped around her. Slowly, Elle found herself doing exactly what he told her to. She closed her eyes and started to bite down on the arm. But as she was being taken farther away from the window, she eventually felt her jaw loosen-up.

When Elle was able to open her eyes, she saw the campsite getting smaller and smaller as she floated in midair.

"What in the world!" she flustered with panic.

Elle wanted to look up but the altitude made her head spin, and she found herself losing consciousness before she was able to see the face of the person holding her.

§

It had been a long time since Elle had had good dreams. On rare occasions, she'd dreamed that she was soaring free as a bird, high up in the clouds where she could ride the wind and soak in the heavens.

When Elle woke up, she found herself inside a small, elegant room. It had dark wood furniture, maroon curtains, and crown moldings that framed the walls.

Instinctively, Elle got out of bed and pressed her ear against the door. She held the doorknob that led to God-knows-where. She was just thinking that it might be safer for her to jump out the window when she heard voices coming from the other side of the door.

"Do you think she can take it?" asked a muffled male voice.

"Well, there's only one way to find out," the other male voice said.

Elle quickly tiptoed toward the window and quietly slid the curtains open. She looked out the window and found vines clinging to the outer walls. She checked if it was sturdy before sliding out of the window and descending as fast as she could.

From the window above her, a guy's head appeared. "I can't believe you're trying to escape from us!" he shouted. "I mean, seriously, people have tried to break *into* this place and you're here, running away!"

Elle tilted her head up and unwittingly saw past the man's face. The skies above him were different. It was far more beautiful than seeing the Milky Way or maybe even the Aurora Borealis. Just leaning back and seeing it made her jolt with surprise, and her grip gave way. The next thing she knew, she was sliding off and was falling fast.

The man quickly leaped out of the window, fire blazing from his shoulder blades as he reached down, catching her halfway from the ground.

"Woah there, you're all right now," he said as he held her close. "What's up with you and falling off of houses? We should really stop meeting like this."

"Mike? Is that you?" Elle looked so stunned that it made Mike smile even more. Elle's eyes grew wide when she saw large red wings hanging out from his back.

"About that, I know you're weirded out right now—that's very normal. But for the record, I've always wanted to say this." Mike switched to his serious voice. "Elle, I welcome you to Eden."

Still cradled in his arms, Elle looked upward. There it was, the grandest of skies any person could ever see. The blue sky blended upward like a gradient into space. Even though it was broad daylight, there were star clusters and numerous unfamiliar planets in various colors and sizes peeping through the clouds. Violet, blue, and pink streaks adorned the sky. It was like the day and night and the universe were one. The view was so odd and surreal that it took her breath away. Directly below it, she saw majestic parcels of land floating in midair with rocks and roots hanging from underneath. Elle could see ponds, full to the brim, their water overflowing, sprinkling the odd-shaped vibrant-colored flowering plants and gigantic trees.

She gazed at the mountains towering over the horizon like beacons of glory. Below them, the lakes glistened, filled with the most beautiful hues that mirrored the sky. Even the fresh scent in the breeze carried love and comfort that she has never felt before.

Everything seemed alive. The experience of being there was beyond words, like a dream that felt all too real. Elle blinked, realizing that she was in the arms of a boy whose deep green eyes stared closely at her.

PART II: *REVELATIONS*

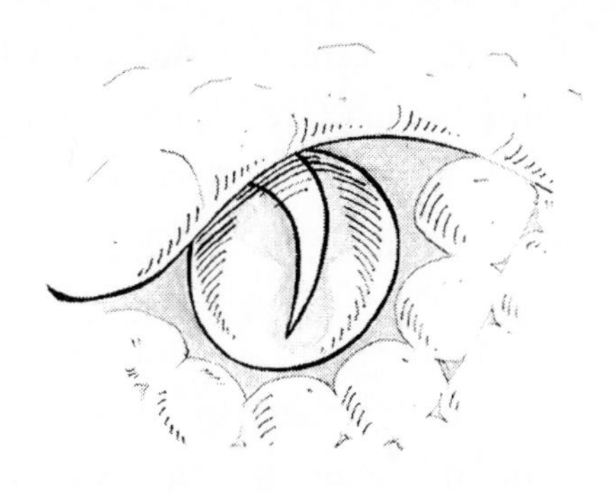

CHAPTER FOUR

- Elle -

Mike held her close. “Sorry, where are my manners? That one over there is Amos, and I believe you’ve already met Erin,” he said as he lifted her up toward a balcony.

Elle turned her attention to the balcony where she saw a man smiling widely as he waved hello. He had dreadlocks and—Elle gulped—was shirtless. The last part made her very uncomfortable but she couldn’t take her eyes away from the tattoos on his tanned skin. They were ancient-looking symbols, like hieroglyphs.

Erin was there, too. She stood beside the tattooed man, looking like an elven queen. “I hope you’re alright, Elle,” she said. “Come, we’ve prepared a meal for you.”

There were two pairs of pearly white, feathered wings on Erin’s back. She was sure there were *two pairs* because she counted—*one, two, three, four wings*. Erin had a double set that was gracefully tucked in behind her.

Elle blinked. It took her a while to register everything that she was seeing. “You’re the student council president,” Elle said as she hopped down onto the balcony with Mike. “I’m feeling really lightheaded right now.” She rubbed her temples. “So really, was I drugged? Am I dead? How did I get here?”

Her barrage of questions came to a sudden halt when she got a whiff of the sweet homey scent of freshly baked bread. At the center of the balcony was a garden table that had fresh fruits, pancakes, some bread and butter, and pitchers of orange juice and milk. Her stomach growled in hunger.

Amos pulled out a chair for her. "You don't look drugged or dead. Just really flushed and zombie-ish," he said jokingly.

She looked around her before taking a seat. Above them were purple jade vines that hung from the beams. The balcony railings were made of wrought iron with an outline that took the shape of wings. And beyond that was nothing less than a breathtakingly surreal landscape.

"Elle," Mike said, his voice full of concern. "You're going to need your strength and some color on that face." He then handed her some bread and butter. "Also, you got here because we saved you."

"I can't believe this is happening. I think I'm about to wake up any moment now." Elle closed her eyes and opened them again.

"Hah!" blurted Amos. "I assure you, we are as real as it gets!"

"If you are," commented Elle, "then that man in Big Ben's office, the Grandmaster, was he real too? I don't think so."

Mike held her hand. "He is as real as you. He just happens to be ancient. We have reason to believe that Wichpot works for him and the two of them must have been conniving on fishing you out."

"I don't get it. What could they possibly want from me?" Elle said, her voice failing her. "And that man, it felt as if he was controlling me."

"He did," Mike said. "You'll actually need to learn how to block it."

Before Elle could react, she realized that Mike's hand was still on hers. Embarrassed, she quickly retrieved it and took a bite of her bread.

"I don't know, you can't expect me to just believe all this," she said.

Amos cleared his throat, noticing the awkwardness between the two. "Alright then. Let's start with a few things that you *can* believe. Look around you. What do you see?"

"Okay. Right now I'm seeing feathery wings behind your backs," replied Elle, "How is that possible?"

Amos was scratching his head when Erin jumped in. She must have noticed how he was having a hard time finding the right words. She gave Elle a proud, elf-like smile, "being able to transcend is all about advanced evolution," she said. "It's because Midians had to adapt to the needs of our time."

"So these Midians," Elle echoed. "Are they like a mutation of some alien race?"

Erin gave a lighthearted laugh. "Not at all. We're the same as you, except for the fact that we were able to develop at a faster rate."

"Hmmm," Elle pondered out loud, "so it's more like your people were able to adapt to the conditions here in Eden that it somehow made you evolve faster. I'm surprised—it's starting to make a lot of sense."

"I'm glad that you're taking things fairly well," Erin said. "About Midians, it's the term we call the people of Eden and just like in your world, we also belong to different races. The Sky Dwellers, like us, are people who can transform into feathered creatures. Most people consider our hybrid form as angels. Then there's the Land Dwellers. They are the ones who can transform into certain animals found on land and have hybrid forms such as centaurs, fauns, and the like. Sea Dwellers, on the other hand, can transform into merpeople and sea creatures. And then, there's the Wanderers."

"I'm actually looking forward to seeing what they're like. I think it's quite exciting," Elle said. "The last one you mentioned, the Wanderers. What are they?"

Erin gave Mike a concerned look.

"You see," Mike said. "Wanderers take the form of reptiles and are definitely not the 'nicest.' They are beings that are greatly conflicted, confused, and misunderstood. You won't see them here anymore, especially since the banishment. They are the most cunning and dangerous of all. They have the power to dissuade man with poisonous words and sorcery. As cold-blooded individuals, their ways are much different from ours."

Elle found herself gripping her utensils tightly as she continued to listen.

"They have the ability to see people's auras," Mike said. "And most of them dwell on the negative aura, making them see the deepest evil in people. Reptiles who have been overcome by darkness have a distorted view of the world. When you look at them straight in the eye, in their pupils, you'll see your reflection turned upside down. They'll try to draw out the darkness from within every person they encounter. This is why pleasantries and kindness are hard to come by but not entirely impossible."

The hair on Elle's arms stood and she had to gulp down a glass of orange juice.

"Is everything alright, Elle?" Mike asked.

"Yes. I'm fine. It's just… I've been having nightmares, and it was just like that. Reptile-like monsters with eyes that have inverted reflections."

"You've dreamed of them?" Erin asked.

Elle blinked. "Yes. I didn't want to sleep because of them. Now you tell me that they're real. That there's no escaping them except being here in Eden."

Erin leaned forward. "By any chance, were you able to find a way to defeat them?"

"No," she replied. "I never get to beat them in my dreams."

Erin turned to Mike with a concerned expression. "I'm sure we'll figure things out sooner or later."

"For now," Mike said, "finish your food. Afterwards, we're going to head east and pay someone a visit."

"Sure. Who are we visiting?" Elle asked.

Mike grinned. "You'll see."

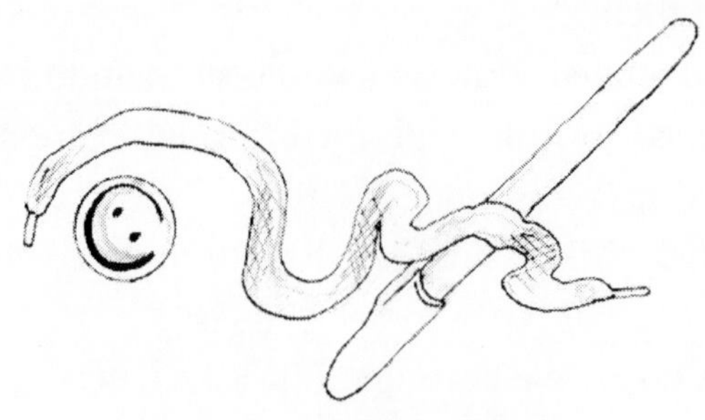

CHAPTER FIVE

- Mike -

Mike escorted Elle through the hallways of the castle to the room she woke up in so she could get ready before they headed out.

"I'll be in the other room," Mike said. "Don't go hopping off the window now!"

Elle laughed. "Yeah, I won't."

Mike adored the sound of her laughter. It somehow burrowed right through him. He stepped back and nodded courteously as she closed the door.

From across the hallway, Mike saw Erin approach him.

"Still the same old Mike," Erin said when she passed by him. "We've been looking out for her for over a year now, and we both know her effect on you. Having her around is going to distract you from your duties. Keep your head straight, okay? For all of our sakes."

Mike did not reply nor react to her accusation and just kept his stance. When she left, he opened the door across Elle's room.

Big Ben's study was huge. On the left side of the room were a desk and a wall with a huge map of Eden. In the middle were pedestals that held artifacts, scrolls, and prototypes of his father's experiments. On the right side was a maze of bookshelves that you could, in fact, get lost in. He considered leaving the door open so he could keep an eye out toward the hallway.

Mike walked across the marble floor and opened the window of the study. He leaned out and peered at the sky. The weather had been erratic for the past few days, and it looked like today was going to be forgiving.

He had been sitting on the windowsill when Elle emerged from the doorway.

"Omigosh!" Elle exclaimed when she entered the study. "Is that an actual trident?"

She hurried over to one corner where a golden trident stood.

"It is," he replied. "They are called Whiloms. They're items that are meant to help Midians fulfill their duties. There are only a few of these in circulation because the Steele family had stopped producing them, whereas the remaining ones are being regulated by the elders. These Whiloms are here because my father is one of the pillars of Eden. That's why he is tasked to protect some of them."

"I see. So, this is like a Sea Dweller's Whilom? I think I read about my grandpa, trying to find Whiloms from his journal," Elle said.

"I didn't know he had a journal," Mike said. He would actually like to read it one day, but it felt wrong to ask. "Do you want to know a bit more about Sea Dwellers?"

"Of course I do," she replied.

"Okay, so there once was a Merman named Alon. He was one of the great pillars of Eden. He had devised a way to protect and hide the sea creatures by creating different kinds of camouflage and illusions."

"That's amazing!" Elle exclaimed, admiring the trident.

Mike nodded. "More than that, during the uprising, this man also founded a place where he kept merpeople and sea creatures hidden, concealed from the eyes of non-sea dwellers."

"Wait, are you telling me that Atlantis exists?" she asked. "That it's here in Eden?"

"Yes," he replied. "That's exactly it."

"That is totally mind-blowing!" Elle cried out. She looked like she was going to ask more about it when something else caught her eye.

"What about that one?" she asked, pointing at the huge golden ring that floated above the intricately designed podium. "Is that a Whilom, too?"

Mike nodded. "That's a Sky Dweller's Whilom. We place that over our heads to become invisible—the same way certain Sea Dwellers use their tridents."

"IT'S A HALO!" Elle gasped.

Mike stifled a laugh. "Umm, yeah. We actually call it a Sphere."

Elle blinked. "Wait, you become invisible when you wear it? Have you ever used that to spy on people – or me specifically?"

"I haven't earned my Sphere yet," he said. "But I will be worthy of it. Someday, when I'm ready."

Mike thought about his mother as he took one last look at the Sphere. To him, it was a poignant reminder of what he never had.

"We probably should get going. This way," he said, pointing toward the heap of tall bookshelves.

Elle nodded, "Uhm, Mike?"

"Yeah?"

"Is it okay if I take a closer look at your wings?"

"Go ahead," he said. Mike turned around to give Elle a full view of his wings that had crimson red feathers.

Mike felt her soft warm hands against his back as she dug both hands beneath the plumes. His muscles quivered the moment she touched the part where his wings were connected to his back, partially touching his skin.

"They feel so real," she whispered.

Mike turned to face her, "Yup, they are."

He didn't know how to act around her so he ended up using his right wing to tickle her cheek.

Elle smiled and looked at him in awe. Mike wanted to tell her how beautiful she looked when she gets all excited, but decided not to. He had no idea how she'd react.

Instead, he continued to lead her through the maze full of books until they reached a stone-walled gallery that led to the garden where they could see the rim of the land.

"Your house is just up there," Mike said as he pointed to a distant house that sat on a hovering parcel of land. "I'll take you there after we drop by the east side."

"Wait," she said. "You mean I'm going to live there? Seriously? On that floating house?"

"Yeah, we're neighbors, apparently," he said. "So, would you like me to carry you or would you prefer learning to fly?"

"No, no, no," she gasped. "I think we both know that I can't."

Mike walked out further. "Well, then I hope you believe in fairies."

"Can't we just walk?" she pleaded.

"Consider this a tutorial," Mike said. He closed his eyes and began to summon a fellow guardian. "Koinonia Aeris," he whispered.

A burst of wind and mist swept along the garden and before them appeared a tiny girl.

Aeris' wings gleamed like that of a dragonfly as she fluttered about. She looked around and started taking a few trinkets she could carry. She gathered a button, a shoelace, and a pen. However, the pen was far bigger than she had hoped. So, she took off the cap, hooked it on her belt and left the pen. She glanced at Elle and flew up close to her face, her tiny hands touching the tip of Elle's nose, making her giggle.

"Her name is Aeris," Mike said. "She'll help you fly."

"Hi," Elle said. "It's nice to meet you."

Aeris whirled around, sprinkling glittery dust on Elle's head until gravity lost its hold on her. Mike smiled because he knew how it felt. It was a mixture of joy, youth, and wonder.

"I think it's working!" Elle exclaimed.

Aeris was teeming with glee as she flew up and nestled on Mike's hair. She tumbled about and did her best to make snow angels on his head. Mike made a comical face and called out to her. "Alright, if you're done messing up my hair, I think it would be very nice if we could get going now."

Aeris slid down his shoulder and nodded cheerfully.

Mike leaped and hovered beside Elle.

"How come you're not flapping your wings, and you're still afloat?" she asked.

"The same reason you're afloat. It's kind of like zero gravity," he said. He reached out to hold her hand and slowly, they rose higher.

"Omigosh! I don't think I can. What if I fall, Mike?"

Elle closed her eyes and clung onto his arm, which made him flinch.

"Are you okay?" she asked, concerned. "Are you injured?"

Elle looked at his arm and recognized the teeth marks. "I'm so sorry! I didn't know that it was you that I bit."

"Don't worry about me," Mike replied. The wound didn't bother him one bit. He was in the moment. He was there with Elle, holding her hand. "I'm fine… Anyway, Aeris and I won't let you fall from the sky. Right Aeris?"

Aeris saluted and gave his pointer finger a fist bump. "Is Aeris a Sky Dweller too?" asked Elle.

"She is. She can also transform into a dragonfly. They usually watch over one particular tree the same way we watch over one particular person.

"I see. Who are you watching over?"

Mike poked Elle on the nose. "This one," he said. "And before I forget, I believe I should be saying the words—tag, you're it!"

Elle's eyes fluttered closed. It took a while before her lips broke into a smile. Hurriedly, she reached out and tagged him back on the forearm. Mike found it impossible to wipe the grin off his face as he watched Elle, with her silver hair gleaming in the sunlight. He could see the thrill and excitement in her bright blue eyes.

In a plot to impress her, Mike went up to a cloud and used his hands to mold it into a rabbit. Elle giggled as she tried to do the same. Aeris, on the other hand, jokingly sat on the cloud-rabbit's back but fell right through. They all burst out laughing.

"Hey, Aeris, want a free ride?" asked Mike.

Aeris nodded triumphantly and sat on his head with her hands clinging tightly on his hair.

"We'll get there real soon," he said to Elle. "By the way, is there anything else you'd like to know about Eden?"

"Actually, yes." she replied. "Can you tell me a little more about how the lands are able to hover above the ground? I think they're absolutely beautiful. The scenery here is like a moving painting."

"I've never heard anyone describe it like that," Mike said as he reminded himself that it was Elle's first time in Eden. "Well, these floating parcels of land are called Gans. They contain aurelle. It's an extremely polarized mineral that allows it to hover above ground like magnets repelling each other. This also generates power for our homes."

"That's pretty convenient," Elle replied.

"Upper Gan is where Sky Dwellers build their homes. Higher Gan, on the other hand, is where our elders live. These lands can only float within central Eden. When you get the chance to wander about, you will notice that the forces of nature are more advanced here compared to what you are familiar with."

"I see," Elle replied.

"Also, I should give you a heads-up. At nighttime, it never gets pitch black. Our moon glows bright, and it also makes most plants luminescent."

"Ooh, I'll look forward to seeing that," Elle replied, grinning.

CHAPTER SIX

- Elle -

They lowered down onto a meadow on top of a hill.

"Are you sure it's here?" asked Elle. She looked around, but there was nothing there, not even a house.

Mike sat on a nearby rock. "Yes. Definitely."

The only thing Elle saw was the thick forest that surrounded the hill. At the center of it was a tree, a Great Basin Bristlecone Pine. She recognized it because it had a semblance to the 5,000-year-old tree she had just seen, but this one was healthier and livelier. It had a welcoming fresh scent and a triad of huge trunks that whimsically spiraled and intertwined, forming a hollow in the middle. Its fruits and pinecones were bluish and had lush deep-green colored leaves that rustled as the warm breeze continued to whistle in her ear.

"Is that you, Uriel?" spoke a melodic woman's voice.

Elle stepped back in shock.

"I have waited for you for some time now…" the voice said.

Elle tilted her head sideways. "Where are you?"

No answer.

Elle continued to walk closer to the tree and went inside the nook cocooned in the middle. She reached out to one of its branches and felt a surge of energy. Her knees gave way and she found herself kneeling and crying on the ground. The tree felt warm to the touch and somehow, she knew—she had touched something sacred. She felt bare as she started lifting up all her unspoken truths. She had never cried so openly before and she couldn't stop them from falling. Hot tears just continued to stream down her face and it suddenly dawned on her how very real the world of Eden was.

Elle felt a huge lump in her throat as she lay down on the ground. Her eyes lingered on the exquisite branches that spiraled around her. Attached to them were blue luminescent fruits.

"I see you're curious about my fruits," the tree said.

"I guess. Who are you?" Elle asked.

"I am the Tree of Life," the tree replied.

"What? Oh, then those fruits are forbidden to eat. Well, that's what they say," replied Elle as fast as she could utter them. She sat up and saw that Mike was on guard, watching her every move.

"Besides," she continued saying. "I'm a nobody."

"I see," the tree said. "Just as foretold." The Tree briefly addressed Mike. "No need to fret Mike. She is a Sky Dweller. You see, dear, only a Sky Dweller could refuse to eat the fruit that only I could produce. And on the contrary—you are far from being a nobody."

Elle noticed how Mike valiantly bowed to the tree before sitting back down.

"Me? A Sky Dweller?" Elle gasped.

"Yes," it replied. "Just like Mike over there."

She began to observe Mike. "Is he like the protector of the Tree of Life?" asked Elle. "The cherubim with the sword of fire that turned in all directions?"

"That cherubim was the boy's mother," the tree said. "He never met her. Do you know how a Phoenix gives birth?"

"From the ashes comes new life?" she replied quietly. "So his mom had to die in order to give birth to him." Elle felt her heart sink as she thought about the idea of never getting to meet your own mother.

"Precisely," the tree said. "There can only be one Phoenix in one lifetime. And like Mike and his mother, you too, I believe, will be carrying the weight of the world the same way your grandfather Adam did."

"Wait," Elle blinked. "Are you telling me that my grandfather is THE Adam?"

"I thought you would have figured that out by now," replied the tree. "Your grandparents were the first apes to evolve, my dear. Here in Eden, an animal can transcend into a Midian. You, a human, can transcend into a Midian as well. To transcend is to find your truest self."

Elle was speechless after hearing those words.

"You are Uriel," the tree continued saying. "You are a testament of hope. It is said that Eden will be restored by a Sky Dweller born from the direct line of Adam, that you would be able to fulfill the duties that your forefathers had failed to accomplish."

Elle shook her head and dashed out of the tree through a slit on its trunk. "I'm sorry, but there must be some kind of mistake."

"Uriel…" the tree said, hushing her. "It is no mistake that you were able to resist my fruit. That is proof that you are indeed a Sky

Dweller. Do not doubt yourself."

Elle didn't know what to say. Everything was happening so fast.

"Only by trusting your instincts will you be able to acquire Eve's four Whiloms before it's too late," the tree said.

CHAPTER SEVEN

- Mike -

Mike saw Aeris fly up to Elle. The fairy wiped a tear from Elle's cheek, then she took a strand of hair that was on her shirt and tied it together with the other trinkets.

Elle's eyebrows furrowed, "Really, Aeris? Your timing is remarkable. Would I get a wish if I handed you my tooth?" Elle said petulantly.

Mike sensed the distress in her voice. "We better start heading back now," he said.

"Alright, Michael," the tree said. "But before you leave, I'll give you one leaf to heal that wound of yours. Now, Elle, we'll see each other again soon. I'm sure you have many questions left unanswered."

"I'm sorry for acting up," Elle said, as she tried to steady her breathing. "I'm still at a loss for a reason, but it was an honor meeting you."

"Then I will see you again soon. Le-Ovedah," the tree said.

It took a while before Elle recalled what *Le-Ovedah* meant. She had read about it from one of her grandpa's books. It meant that man is not the owner of the earth. That we are meant to look after it.

Aeris fluttered about and sprinkled glitter on Elle's head.

As Elle started to float, Mike saw her dig into her pocket, taking out a hairclip and a piece of candy. She had accidentally pulled out her keychain flashlight, but she quickly pocketed it back.

"Hey, Aeris, this is all I have on me," she said as she handed over the hairclip and the candy. "It was a pleasure to meet you, too."

Aeris happily hugged her and accepted her peace offering, briskly depositing the gifts in a crevice of the tree.

Mike and Elle hovered before gradually ascending into the clouds.

"Wow," Elle said. "I can't believe I just spoke with the Tree of Life, and she's a woman. How about the Tree of Knowledge? Do we visit him too? Oh wow, I think I just assumed his gender. Maybe it's 'coz they're like reflections of man and woman."

"What do you mean?" he asked.

"I think women could be like a symbol of life for their ability to deliver a child while men are symbols of logic. I don't know, maybe I'm just overthinking it."

"Yes, maybe you are. And the Tree of Knowledge actually went missing. He just vanished."

"How can a Tree go missing? Oh! Wait a second," Elle said. "The Tree spoke about Eve's four Whiloms. They're probably the same one's mentioned in my grandfather's journal."

"Most likely," Mike replied. "I'd also have to tell you more about Eve, your grandmother. Maybe tomorrow when you've had some rest?"

"Yes. That would mean so much to me!" Elle said.

Mike and Elle traveled a lot faster as they headed back using the same route from which they had come.

They landed on top of a gan, where a quaint yellow stone house greeted them. Blue and red wildflowers studded the undergrowth, and there was a small pond along the right side of the house with water that spilled from its rim, glistening as it drizzled onto the trees on the ground below it.

"You're home, safe and sound," he said.

"Thanks, Mike," Elle replied.

Just as Mike was about to turn and leave, Elle blurted out, "Wait a minute! We have to do something about that wound."

"Don't worry about it," He assured her. "I got a leaf from the Tree, remember?"

He took out the leaf, squeezed it in his hand and placed it on top of the wound. "Money doesn't grow on trees, but healing does."

Elle's eyes grew wide as the wound closed up like nothing ever happened.

"Omigosh! It's totally gone!"

"Yeah, you can stop poking my arm now," Mike said, smiling at her. "Well, I had better head off."

"Alright," replied Elle. "I wouldn't want to delay you with what you have to do. Although, am I going to see you tomorrow?"

Before Elle could say another word, Mike took her hand and kissed it.

"It was an honor being your guardian," he said. "I'll be back in a day or two. I think we need to get you in shape if you're going to fight alongside us Sky Dwellers."

Elle walked toward the front door after Mike had left. But halfway there, she heard rustling noises from the bushes.

PART III:
THE UNTOLD STORY

CHAPTER EIGHT

- Elle -

"He's cute, that boy," a tiny voice said.

"Who's there?" Elle cried out nervously.

Out from the bushes jumped a furry squirrel. "Hi, you must be Elle."

"Umm. Yes, I am," Elle said. "And you're talking! I can't believe I'm talking to squirrels now. It's like everything here can talk!" Elle instantly regretted saying that out loud. "I'm sorry. I must sound weird. You're a really cute squirrel, though. Would it be okay if I carry you?"

The squirrel tried to reach upward, but it ended up tumbling backward.

"Oh! You're so adorable!" Elle picked her up and cuddled the squirrel. "What's your name, little squirrel?"

"The name's Willow. And I'm not *just* a squirrel, I'm a *flying* squirrel!" she said proudly. "And those are my friends."

Elle looked over her shoulder. There on the grass was a cricket and a bird. "Oh dear! Okay, you two, come over here."

Up they went to join Willow in Elle's arms.

"Hi, I'm Finchy Jr., son of Finchy Sr.," the bird said, bowing his head. “My dad and I are well-known giant finches around here!”

“Well then,” replied Elle. “It’s very nice to meet you, Finchy Jr. I just don’t know what you mean by giant,” Elle noted with a chuckle.

She turned to the other animal. “And what is your name, little cricket?”

“The name’s Kick. I may be small, but between these two, I’m the most mature,” replied the cricket.

The three critters were all ecstatic and started chatting all at the same time. Elle couldn’t possibly catch up. She decided to carry them with her inside the house. Upon entering, the little ones each picked out their own spot in different corners of the room.

“My goodness, Elle,” her mom exclaimed. “I know they’re nice and all, but you didn’t have to bring them inside.”

“Mom!” Elle squealed and ran up to hug her. “I’m so happy you’re here!”

“My dear,” Emilia said as she hugged her back. “You had us all so worried. Is the Phoenix not joining us? I’ve prepared a nice meal for us. I also wanted to thank him for bringing you here.”

“Yeah, I think he has important things to do,” replied Elle.

“Very well,” her mom said. “Have a seat, young lady. You must be thirsty, ‘coz you look absolutely awful. Here you go,” Emilia said as she flicked her hand toward a pitcher. A stream of water began to float. It made a couple of loops and then it slid into a glass. She handed it to Elle with a picture-perfect smile.

“Uh… what just happened?” Elle asked in disbelief.

“Oh honey,” replied her mom. “I’m a Sea Dweller. We can do all sorts of things.”

“Umm okay,” she said, trying to process things. “Where’s Dad? Is he out?”

Her mom sighed. “Yeah, he’s been busy.”

Elle’s eyes wandered a little, taking in her surroundings. The simple furniture had nice white and aqua blue colors. Not too shabby. In fact, it was perfect!

"Grandpa asked me to add those silly terrariums," her mom said.

"Why? Is he unable to enter Eden?" Elle asked.

Her mom shook her head. "For some reason, when you were born, you opened the gates for our family to enter. Well, all except for your grandfather, which is strange."

"I really wish he was here right now," Elle said sullenly.

"I do too. Every Land Dweller in Eden wishes that."

"Mom, I just met the Tree of Life today and I'm still a little confused. If Grandpa's a Land Dweller and you're a Sea Dweller, how could that possibly make me a Sky Dweller?" Elle asked.

Emilia patted her hand. "Our family lineage has all been Land Dwellers and Sea Dwellers up until you were born. Each individual transcends into who they are. That means, being a part of a specific race isn't dependent on genes."

"Oh. Okay," replied Elle.

"It was on that day," Emilia said, "that the Tree of Knowledge went ablaze and revealed that you are to be a Sky Dweller."

Elle was taken aback. "But I haven't changed yet. What happens if that's not who I really am? What is it they're expecting me to do?"

Deep inside, Elle knew that she wanted to make her family proud. However, she was well aware of her own limitations. Whatever she had to do, she felt like she was already failing them.

Elle tried to regain her composure. "I'm sorry, mom. It's just really a lot to take in."

"Let's just eat before the food gets cold," Emilia said. "I have to head out in a short while anyway."

"You're leaving?" Elle said through a mouthful of salad.

"Don't worry dear. Your father and I will be back by tomorrow afternoon. We just need to procure a couple of things," her mom said.

"Okay, Mom," replied Elle. "'Coz I don't even know how to get down from an Upper Gan."

"We'll be able to help her with those things," the cricket said, butting in.

"Well now," Emilia said, "I'm liking this cricket!"

Elle tilted her head. "Wait a minute, Mom, if you're a Sea Dweller, then how were you able to get up here?"

"Simple," said her mom as she cleared the plates. "The same way I'm going down. Come, I'll show you."

Elle, together with Willow, Kick, and Finchy Jr., followed Emilia as she walked out of the house and lounged in the pond like it was the most comfortable place on earth. She watched in amazement as her mother's legs transformed into a glittery mermaid tail! The pond water began to rise, splashing water on Elle and her friends. A wave formed and carried her mother afloat. "I'll be home before you know it," she said. Emilia blew a kiss and dove into the water as it supernaturally carried her down to the Lower Gan.

"You and your mom are very pretty," Willow said as she shook off the water from her fur. "Except for the fact that she looks prettier drenched in water."

Elle giggled. "Ha! Look who's talking, Ms. Wet Furball!"

They all laughed as they entered the house. She decided to make sure her new friends were dry before she took a good long bath. A warm bath and some comfortable clothes later, she lay down in the bed and fell asleep almost instantly.

§

The next day, Elle got up from bed and sleepily walked straight into a wall.

"Oh jeez!" she exclaimed, softly rubbing the part of her forehead that hit the wall.

Elle sat back down and looked around, still a bit groggy. It took a few seconds before she realized that she wasn't in her old room. The walls were yellow, and there was a bird, a cricket, and a flying squirrel on the bed.

She blinked and tried to remember her dream. All she could recall was how her grandfather had stood facing a dragon.

Something welled up inside her, and she couldn't help but worry. Knowing herself, she had to get her hands busy to clear her head. She looked around and noticed the house was in need of cleaning.

Willow, Kick, and Finchy were nice enough to help her do some chores. It made cleaning more fun. Elle felt like Snow White, minus the singing. Well, she did hum her grandfather's favorite song, *The Story of the Lost Halo*, but that was it.

While having breakfast, Kick suggested a brilliant idea.

"You know, Elle," the cricket said. "Finchy can fly you out of here if you want to go explore Eden."

"He can do that?" she asked, dumbfounded. Elle turned toward the finch. "Finchy, can you really take us?"

"Of course I can. Why is it so hard to believe?" Finchy exclaimed.

"Now now, Finchy," Willow said, feeling sorry for Elle. "You know she's not from around here."

"True," Kick said. "Elle, how about we take you to see your grandparent's old hut?"

Elle's eyes gleamed with anticipation as she forked through what was left on her plate. "That would mean so much to me!"

"Then, to the south we go!" Kick exclaimed.

Elle got ready. In her pocket was her flashlight keychain. In her bag, she carried a pack of dried fruits and nuts, some extra clothes, and her grandfather's journal.

"Alright! I'm all set!" Elle said. "Where's Finchy?"

"He's already out to warm up his wings," Kick said.

The flying squirrel and the cricket started to dash for the front door.

Elle looked out the window just as she was about to leave. Her jaw dropped. There was a giant finch the size of a car outside the house.

Elle ran out to see the bird up close. "Omigosh! Is that you, Finchy?"

The bird was perched on the Upper Gan, making the land tilt to one side.

"Whoops!" Finchy said, "Didn't mean to do that."

Elle ran up to him and hugged Finchy. "This is amazing! You can actually grow at will."

"But I already told you that I was a giant!" Finchy said as he lowered his tail feathers for them to climb up on, "Now hop on! We wouldn't want storm clouds catching up to us."

Elle climbed up his tail and sat on his back. Once they were all settled, Finchy spread his wings and started flying.

"Just so you know," Finchy said. "Right now, we're at the heart of Eden where the Upper and Higher Gans are. On the north side is where the flying squirrels and the deer folk have recently migrated to. Bulbutton Square is to the south. It's where most Land Dwellers live. To the east, you'll find the Tree of Life. Farther east is a huge body of water where Atlantis should be. On the west, well, there's nothing there but a dessert. You won't find creatures there."

"Thank you, Finchy. I bet you're pretty good with directions."

"Ya' got that right!" he replied.

They had been flying above the trees for some time already when Elle noticed a village brimming with life. She could see Land Dwellers strolling along the plaza and some vendors along the side streets. The gigantic trees had carvings on its inside that resembled homes. She could see round windows with half-moon windowpanes along the trunk and round doors at the bottom.

They descended onto the plaza beside a statue of a huge mouse-like figure.

Elle was in awe of how otherworldly the place looked. There were goat-people selling jars of milk in one corner and a lovely family of zebras in another. Before wandering around, she read the inscription at the foot of the statue.

"That is Jon Bulbutton," Willow said with pride in her voice. "Such a kind and hardworking capybara he is. Sadly, he never got to transcend even though he's had such immense contributions to the Land Dwellers."

"I see he founded this place," added Elle. "Although, that's a very curious thing to say, about never transcending. Maybe he just didn't need to. Maybe he was already at the pinnacle of his being. Perfect in itself to simply be a capybara."

"That capybara is a visionary," replied Willow. "He protected the trees and made villages for us where the only things allowed to be cut down are branches, never the trunk."

Elle nodded approvingly; she did see how huge the branches were. It was practically the size of a regular trunk.

Finchy had shrunk back to his regular size and was complaining under his breath about how heavy Elle was. Kick, on the other hand, was just his usual self as he hopped on Elle's shoulder.

"We can go around the village if you want. Your grandparent's house is just a little walk outside Bulbutton Square."

"Oh, yes! Then we should go there," replied Elle.

They passed by the market and some homes until they found themselves in the forest, away from the buzzing sounds of Bulbutton Square.

After a while, Elle saw a tree house that had a rope ladder dangling from it.

"Here we are," Willow said as she climbed up the rope ladder ahead of them.

When Elle reached the entrance of the tree house, she stood up very slowly, making sure the floor wasn't going to crumble under her feet. The porch of the tree house was small, and upon checking the door, she noticed that there was no lock.

She went inside.

The place smelled of cider. The furniture was simple and made of wood. In the middle of the room was the wide tree trunk.

Elle went snooping around. She wanted to know more about her family. Maybe there was a clue in here somewhere. All she knew was that her grandpa was a good lawyer. Then she started to wonder, *Did he just wake up one day and say, I really ought to be a lawyer?* People said that lawyers were a bunch of liars who thought themselves better and smarter than everybody else. Her grandfather, on the other hand, had the humility like no other lawyer that had ever lived, and won because of it. He had kept his center. Elle admired this solid foundation—like he was unbreakable. It was as if her grandpa had tapped into a power source that allowed him to defeat the strongest of men and the foulest of liars. They all seemed to melt and break at the face of his wisdom. For people who really knew him, however, they saw him as a man who was good at doing simple acts of kindness. For Elle, there was something more to it because simple acts of kindness are not so simple.

Genuine kindness requires strength. Genuine kindness

requires love. Genuine kindness requires sacrifice. Sure, he was earning big, but his heart was all the richer. Often, she would see him carry out simple everyday chores as if the act in itself was but a humble prayer. She would listen to him talk and sing while they tended to the garden, and it was those moments that she cherished the most.

Elle was about to walk across the tree house to check out the bedroom when she found herself frozen in place. Right in front of her was a desk with a sketch portrait of two apes holding each other with eyes as vivid as reality itself. Elle's hands squeezed the frame as she endeavored to recognize her own grandfather in another form. This was that side of him that she never got to know.

Elle started opening crates and boxes. Her heart kept pounding as she turned the place upside-down. She felt miffed for having been cheated and kept away from the truth. She needed to know and uncover the story that had been kept from her for so long. Then, inside one of the crates, she chanced upon a brunette woman's portrait. This must be Eve. She looked beautiful and had a smile that lingered somewhere deep inside her eyes. Elle set the parchment aside, and she saw another sketch amongst the stack. It was the drawing of a dragon.

Elle took out her grandfather's journal. Maybe when she gets to talk to her grandpa again, she'd be able to finally ask him about everything she wanted to know. And yet there it was—that feeling of worry that just kept burying itself inside of her.

She browsed the pages again, but she couldn't understand a thing written on it. She took a deep breath and slumped hopelessly flat on the floor among the scattered books and sketches. *Maybe I just need some air.* She left the three critters to get some rest as they napped on top of the scattered papers.

Elle went out carrying the journal and sat on a rickety chair that she found along the front porch. Dark clouds were starting to form as Elle watched the horizon from atop the tree house. She took out a piece of cloth from her bag and wrapped the journal so that it wouldn't get soaked. Just as she finished wrapping it, Elle heard a loud swoosh.

An arrow had swooped near her, snagging the journal away. It fell onto the grass below. Elle quickly ducked her head. She was able to find a fissure on the floor and as she peered through it, she saw that the journal was missing.

She listened for a moment until she heard something move among the bushes.

"Hey! Stop! That's mine!" she cried out.

Elle got down from the tree house and ran as fast as she could. Rain was starting to pour.

"Please stop! It's going to get ruined!"

The ground was starting to get slippery while the thick undergrowth continued to lash at her legs. Huge lumps of raindrops also fell square on her face as she ran. From time to time, Elle would catch sight of a pair of antlers moving about. She continued to follow the sound of its movement until it stopped. Elle breathed heavily as she walked out to a clearing.

In front of her stood a tall woman. The first thing Elle noticed was the pair of antlers on her head. She had a few beaded braids in her brunette hair. Peering out of the sides were pointy ears. She wore a white toga that had blue ethnic patterns, and she had on a necklace that held a vial in place. Under it, her chest was flat. Slightly visible from her side were old wounds in place where her breast should be. The woman held a bow on her left hand and the journal on her right. She stood still like a stalk of bamboo, her eyes glowing like the moon.

"Give it back…" Elle muttered as she walked closer.

The woman dropped her bow and pulled out the book.

"Young girl, this does not belong to you," the woman said, her voice reverberating.

"Yes, it's my grandfather's," explained Elle.

"You are that girl, Uriel. I know. But this is not just any book. Do you even understand the relevance of what is written between these pages?"

"Who are you?" asked Elle. "Are you a friend of my grandfather?"

There was a hint of smile as she spoke. "The name is Luna. And as for your grandfather, he happens to be a friend to everybody. Tell you what. Allow me to train you, and I will ensure your victory. How does that sound?"

"Are you a trainer? Will you be able to help me? Everyone has been saying that I am to be a Sky Dweller." Elle asked.

"I am not a trainer, but it seems I am yet to be. And yes, there is a chance that you may transcend, but it would be difficult. There hasn't been a newborn Sky Dweller in the longest time. Just think of this as my way of thanking Adam for teaching me many things."

"Alright then. I'll have to check with my parents before I take you up on that offer. And by the way, you can call me Elle. Uriel is how my mom calls me when I know I'm in a lot of trouble," Elle replied.

Luna nodded. "Alright. We should get ready."

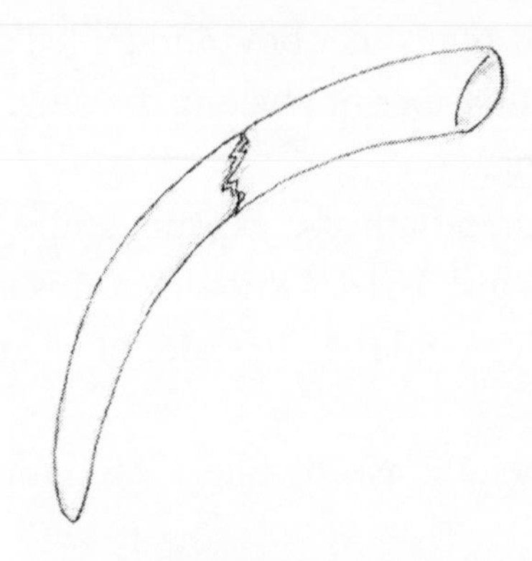

CHAPTER NINE

- Mike -

Mike was beaming as he paced toward Ben Gabriel's office. He couldn't help it. The warmth of Elle's hand still lingered on his skin.

As Mike was about to enter his father's study, he bumped into Sir Boris Steele.

"Oh, hey there, mah boy!" he greeted.

"Boris!" Mike exclaimed as he took the man's hand and bumped their shoulders.

"How's mah old apprentice doing these days?"

"I'm well, but I still have a long way to go."

"Aye, bett'r forget everything I taught ye then. Making weapons, fighting, tactics—might as well just throw it all."

"What are you saying? Why? Wait, are you leaving already?"

"Yeah. Just had to tell yer father someth'n. I'll see ye around, mah boy. Look after yer father, ye hear me?"

"Of course."

"Best ye know, there's someth'n in the wind. And it's up to no good."

Mike watched him leave before walking into the study and saw his father behind his desk.

"I just bumped into Boris. What was it he came here to tell you?"

"It's nothing important. Come, take a look at this," Big Ben said.

On top of the desk, Mike saw a globe that had seven rings swirling around it.

"Hmm... I'm not sure I'm familiar with this planet. Are you scouring it for the demon who calls himself Grandmaster?"

Big Ben readjusted his binocular-like spectacles over the bridge of his nose as his intelligent eyes stared back at him.

"Mike, we need to talk," his father said as he walked away from his desk. "I have good news, son. We'll be able to hunt him down. Thanks to Elle, we were able to put a tracker on him. Only *he* would dare to sit on my chair, so it's him alright."

"You used Elle as a pawn?" Mike asked incredulously.

"It was the only way," his father said. "We are currently devising a trap to get him once and for all."

Mike's joyful mood turned sour.

"Elle deserved better than that," he said firmly. "I won't let you do anything like that again."

His father sighed.

"I know. It was a desperate move," Big Ben said as he turned around and latched his sword onto his waist. It was the Sword of Wrath, a weapon that had belonged to his wife, Mike's mom, the cherubim. It was dubbed as the flaming sword, but as an owl, it has never gone ablaze in his father's hands. It was because he wasn't a phoenix like Mike and the cherubim.

"Also, it's about time for you to have this," Big Ben said as he handed a golden Sphere. "You've earned it, son,"

Mike blinked in surprise. In his palms was his mother's Sky Dweller Whilom—the same Sphere that she had used when she single-handedly protected the Tree of Life. It felt heavy and cold as it tingled in his fingertips.

"If things go south," his father said, "I should have at least taught you how to use a Sphere." His father patted his shoulder. "Put it on son. Lesson starts now."

Mike did as he was told. Once he had placed the Sphere on top of his head, he instantly felt lightheaded. A sound rang and echoed in his ear, and when he looked down, he found that his feet were translucent. He tried to lean against the desk but his hand went right through it.

"Relax and breathe deep," his father said before putting on his own Sphere. Upon placing it on his head, Big Ben became ghost-like just like Mike was. "Never forget, Le-Ovedah," his father said. "Come, I want you back here before the sun sets."

Mike followed his father out to the balcony. They flew up to the sky where the day slid into space. Beside them were planets and heavenly bodies. Big Ben floated toward one planet. "Here we are. Now let's be on with it," he said as he dived into the planet.

They started to pick up speed as they entered the atmosphere.

"Now!" shouted Big Ben.

His father opened up his wings and did a backflip just above the clouds. Mike did the same, but an airplane flew so close to him that he fumbled in stretching out his wings and lost control, making him plummet down into the lake like a comet. He was so deep underwater that he could see the seabed.

If this was Sky Dweller Training 101, I think I just failed it, Mike thought.

Mike gasped for air the moment his head popped out of the water. Apparently, he could still pass through water, but he couldn't breathe under it. Once safely on dry land, Mike took his Sphere off.

His father slowly hovered down toward him, sphere in hand.

"Are you alright, son?"

"Sorry, Father," Mike said. "I know that airplane would have just passed through me. But I hesitated."

"You'll get used to it in time," Big Ben said as he extended his hand to help him up.

Mike hadn't noticed it before, but as he got up, he noticed how extremely old his father was. His father had a good built, but aging has made his grip shaky, weaker than it used to be. Mike recalled how he used to always run to him for help, to the man who stood as both his father and mother. A wise, caring, and responsible man. A father who was strict, yet patient. It was probably the exact same reason why he was the perfect Headmaster for Hillworth High.

Mike had always wanted to be more like him, just as everyone at school looked up to him.

He and his father did their regular patrol, but this time, instead of driving around the streets, they were flying invisibly over houses, trying to sense danger and only entering homes when needed. On patrols, they would report cases of violent behavior to the authorities. They would prevent thefts by appearing on side alleys and talking to thieves to set them off their game. Occasionally, they would encounter Wanderers who needed guidance.

When there was no trouble in the air, like today, he and his father would head over to hospitals and orphanages and check on individuals.

As Mike watched the orphans run carelessly around the playground, he couldn't help but recall how silly he had been when he was their age. Back then, he thought it would be fun if he could play cupid once he got his Sphere. He imagined how he'd create happy, first-time, meeting accidents for couples. For some reason, even though he was a phoenix, he still wondered what love was like. It sometimes made him feel sad, knowing that he was a being created without a soulmate.

At sunset, when Mike and Big Ben had finished patrolling, they took the time out and stood at the edge of an apartment building to admire the city splayed before them.

"Son, you see this land?" his father said with a hint of nostalgia. "It's where both light and darkness thrive. In Eden, we do not experience total darkness because our moon glows bright, but here, it is real, and it is everywhere. It covers the land as if you've had your eyes closed for lengths at a time."

His father gave him a serious look. "Whenever you return to Eden from this land, I want you to go to the Tree of Life and request that you be stripped of darkness. As a phoenix, you will bring a great amount of good to this world just like your mother."

Big Ben looked grave. "And about that silver-haired Sky Dweller, Elle. We both know that there's a force hindering her from transcending."

Mike nodded, knowing exactly what he meant. Elle hadn't transcended yet, and she would have to find herself before the imbalance gets worse.

Big Ben breathed in deep.

"We haven't had any new Sky Dweller for almost a decade. But hope is not lost," he said. "Elle may just be the key to fulfilling His plan. Son, when the time comes and when the task proves to be too great, always remember that your mother will always be with you in spirit."

"Yes, father," Mike replied.

"Such a beautiful sunset," Big Ben said. Mike watched him as he closed his eyes and felt the last rays of sun on his face.

"I believe it's time for you to head back, Son. There are matters I need to settle."

Big Ben leaped and transformed into an owl before flying in

the opposite direction of the sun and straight into the dark.

Mike stayed a while longer to watch the stars appear before making his way back to Eden. But not long after, he began to sense an unusual energy.

"No… It can't be."

§

Mike didn't head back. Instead, he rushed in the direction his father had flown and transcended into a phoenix.

His body morphed into a fiery blaze. Large, ferocious, and burning red with flames. He tore his way toward a star-studded sky, leaving a scarlet streak in his wake. Somewhere just ahead, he heard a faint roar as rain sizzled on his back. His heart pounded frantically. He didn't know if his combat training during his apprenticeship with Sir Boris Steele had been enough to prepare him for what was to come.

Up ahead, a colossal dragon was towering above the trees and in front of it was his father, levitating alongside a giant ape. Nearby, other Midians were closing in: three white-winged Sky Dwellers, and about seven horned, furry, lean, and brusque Land Dwellers of different descent. All of them were intent on defeating the fearsome dragon. At the sight of them, the creature started to fly away, flapping its enormous wings. It went straight up before diving towards Mike.

Mike had no choice but to dart left. To his horror, he had glimpsed at the reflection of himself from the dragon's glassy eye. His image had been upside down with a devilish glint in its stare. It shook him, and for some reason, he began to feel doubt within himself. He tried to shake it off and took a deep breath to charge his lungs.

The phoenix unleashed the air from its chest and blasted a whirlwind of fire that struck its side, making the dragon lose altitude. Still unfazed, it continued its trail by flying lower to the ground.

Behind it, the huge ape leaped as high as it could and rammed the dragon. He slammed it to the ground and quickly pinned it down into submission. The dragon struggled, but the ape was determined to win. The brawl grew intense, but eventually, the dragon had stopped moving. It would seem that the vile creature's composure had softened when their eyes had locked on each other. Could it be that the dragon had finally acknowledged the ape's prowess?

"Hold your fire!" shouted Mike.

But it was too late. A minotaur had already thrown an axe with such force that it pierced the dragon's hide. The ape roared at them, but it was too late. The dragon, as if betrayed, instinctively bit the ape.

"No!" screamed Big Ben.

It was the first time Mike had seen his father so enraged. In a split second, his father had thrust out his hand—giving every last bit of himself into his sword.

Next came a tremendous explosion.

Mike felt his body hit the ground. When he regained consciousness, he found himself lying in the middle of the forest in his human form. His vision was hazy and his ears were ringing like a sonic wave had wiped the land. The tree trunks were all bent and the air was filled with flaming sawdust that twinkled in the dark. His body was aching but he continued to stand up, spread out his wings, and fly above the forest to search of his father and the others.

The dragon was nowhere to be found but along the epicenter

he saw a wounded man. Mike hurried to his aid. It was his father.

"Father… Can you hear me?" he said as he checked for signs of life.

"Son…" Big Ben breathed out in pain.

"Hold on, Father," Mike said. "I'm going to take you to the Tree."

"There's no need for that," his father replied as he clutched Mike's hand. "She won't be able to heal me." Big Ben coughed. "Listen to me. I am proud of you. You were really brave fighting off the dragon. I can't believe how much you've grown. You're becoming the phoenix your mother and I knew you could be. Oh, your mother, how I miss her so."

"No. I won't let you give up," Mike said.

He now understood what his father had meant. Earlier, he had been confused when his father had asked him to pray to be stripped of darkness because his father was an owl and owls could see clearly in the dark. As for him, being a phoenix born of fire meant that he could extinguish the dark. He didn't quite realize until now that what his father was referring to was not entirely about the setting of the sun. It was darkness of a different kind, one that took many forms of dark imaginings combined. It was the kind of darkness that could overcome one's heart. The kind of darkness that could consume one's being.

As a Sky Dweller, Mike knew what his father had done. He had cleared the Wanderer's eyes with the gift of light. It was a sacrifice that was enough to take his life.

He did it for Adam, for me, and for all of us.

His father took up the Sword of Wrath, "This is yours now," he said. "Be brave, Son. Be loving. Be good."

Mike's tears welled up. "Father…"

He felt Big Ben squeeze his hand one last time.

Slowly, his arm fell to the side as life left his eyes.

Mike kept his arms around him until he felt the soft wind. It whirled about as Aeris appeared. The fairy looked at Mike sullenly and descended near Big Ben's limp arm. With her tiny arms, she labored to pick-up the Sword of Wrath that was lying beside his father and handed it to Mike.

The moment Mike touched it, the blade went ablaze. The Sword of Wrath was aflame once again in the hands of a phoenix, and at that moment, Mike felt his mother's presence. He kissed his father's forehead. *They are together now*, he thought.

The Midians who had seen Mike and Big Ben were in shock, but somehow the sight of his weapon had sparked hope in their eyes, hope that he could be just as strong as his mother.

"Will the Tree claim him?" Mike asked Aeris.

The fairy nodded gloomily.

The ground reverberated as roots came springing up from the soil. Mike got up and moved back as the roots intertwined and began to enclose his father's body. Everyone was silent. A Pillar of Eden had fallen.

Mike's jaw clenched, and with great force, he shot up in the sky in the same manner his father had flown. The rain drowned out his tears as he scoured the forest. He wanted justice for his father.

He was concentrating on finding the dragon when he sensed two Sky Dwellers tailing him. It was Amos and Erin. Mike didn't want to be consoled, and he made sure his friends knew that too. They reported as they normally would when they caught up with him.

Erin had a grave expression on her face.

"Mike, on our way here, we found Wichpot. She appeared to be running away. Amos and I saw her enter some sort of portal through those hills," she said, pointing to a cracked stone hill.

Amos soared higher and flew next to him. "Mike, if Wichpot works for that Grandmaster, then he must have had a hand in all this chaos with the dragon."

Mike held up a hand to silence his friends. From a distance, he could almost see a person transcending back into a dragon somewhere along a secluded bay.

§

The trees surrounding the bank had already been lit in flames, filling the sky with black smoke as the water glared red with its reflection.

The ape was there. All muddy in front of the dragon.

After a while, the giant ape shrank and transformed into its human form. It was Adam, Elle's grandfather. He was staring up, looking intently between the slits of the dragon's eyes. He looked extremely weak. It was clear that he was an easy prey for the dragon who was now preparing to breathe fire in his direction.

Just in the nick of time, Amos swooped in and took Adam away before the flames thrashed down onto the sand.

"Stand down, old man," Amos said. "I don't think your heart would be able to hold out this battle."

He let Adam rest his back against a tree before flying up to rejoin Mike and Erin.

Mike hovered while Erin and Amos awaited instructions. He knew they had to finish the fight once and for all, but how? Was he meant to kill the dragon?

I need to do this. The world depends on it, Mike thought. As fire wielders, he knew that no matter how much they'd blaze at each other, the two of them would just come out unscathed. That means the dragon would have to come close if it wanted to kill him.

"Let's corner him and form a triangle," Mike said.

He lunged forward and fought the dragon head on while Amos and Erin attacked from different angles. His swift movements spoke of precision and confidence that held the grace and form of a true warrior.

At first, the dragon kept breathing fire at him, but upon realizing that it didn't burn Mike, it started to use force on him. Everything was going as planned. After a few jousts, Mike was starting to see a pattern in the dragon's movements. *This is going to be easier than I thought.* But Mike wasn't the only one reading his opponent.

The dragon roared loudly and in one swift movement, its claws and tail had knocked down Erin and Amos. Mike thought it was going to come after him next, but it didn't. He was still a little stunned when the dragon dove into the water where it knew it had the upper hand.

Mike checked on his friends and sighed with relief. They're going to be alright.

He had underestimated the creature. No. He can't let it escape. But how? There's no way he could fight under water. Before he knew it, a small tugboat was burning along the coastline. *That sneaky dragon!*

He was about to fly off when he saw the water rise into a tide. Other Midians were there. He was sure of it. A wave had washed out the flames and had carried the boat safely near the shore. A powerful Sea Dweller must have done that. Maybe he would get reinforcements after all.

Mike went to check on Adam when a sound distracted him.

It was the sound of someone clapping his hands.

From the shadows, a man appeared.

"I see you've found a new ally," said the man with long white hair and outdated clothes.

"You're that Serpent!" Adam declared. He tried to stand, but he didn't have the strength to lift himself up.

"Oh, yes. I'm simply the one who created the dragon," replied the man. "Poor old Adam. Do you really think that the Creator loves you?" he said, pointing his cane at Adam. "Can you honestly say that you've lived a happy life? That He gave you the happiness that you deserved? You see, I've been watching you. How faithful and good you are. But then again, where did being good take you?"

"It gives me peace," replied Adam.

The man started to laugh, "So, for you, peace is the same as happiness? No, I don't think so, old man. Being good gave you heartache, being good gave you nothing but His burden, being good gave you a life far worse than being a demon. Why can't you admit that He has forsaken you? It's quite sad to see so much talent go to waste. You do have so much potential—all that power you never embraced."

"Well, Serpent," Adam said, "how about you tell me? Did anger and hate help you find the happiness you think you deserve? I'm sure that before you came to be, you've experienced what it's like to find happiness in simple things—that real and genuine happiness. Do you remember it? That 'once upon a time' right before you lost sight of the person you seek? A time when you were your best self, when you had more answers than questions? A time when the epitome of true happiness was actually in 'Becoming,' becoming the person that you want to be? Do you not long for a life that is driven by love? I suggest you look at the world for what it is and even as a Serpent you will see. The Creator is here. He is one and all."

The man's face began to distort with rage. "Give me Eve's four Whiloms, and I will let her go. I know you stole them!"

"He will do no such thing," Mike said as he aimed the Sword of Wrath at the other man. "This is for my father!"

Mike lunged forward, but before he could hit him, the man had vanished into the darkness, leaving only his voice in the air like a lingering hiss.

"Your father died for naught. Eve still belongs to me."

The dragon had once again leaped out of the water and roared.

"No. This ends now," Adam declared.

Just as the Grandmaster disappeared, Mike heard footfalls. He knew the cavalry had arrived right on time.

They were the same Midians who had fought with Adam and his father earlier. For some reason, they seemed to have renewed vigor knowing they were alongside a phoenix who held the Sword of Wrath.

As Mike watched the Midians attack the dragon, he couldn't help but feel as if there was something wrong. Their main opponent was the Grandmaster. He was the one they needed to defeat. Mike wore his Sphere and snuck away. He was invisible as he flew and checked for signs of the Grandmaster.

Mike continued to soar close to the ground when something caught his attention. On the sand, he noticed a red-eyed snake, muttering something that looked and sounded like a binding enchantment. Entwined in the snake's coiled body was a curved bone.

Mike hovered closer. The bone appeared to be a rib. *Could it be? Adam's rib... the one that became a part of Eve!* Mike quickly took off his Sphere and became visible to his opponent. With a mighty swing, he cut the snake's tail and smashed the rib in half.

A second later, the snake lashed out—its poisoned teeth sinking into Mike's ankle before slithering away.

Mike felt the poison burn through his body, but before he

passed out, he was able to catch a glimpse of the dragon imploding. Its breath of fire became fierce as if it had burned its body from the inside. Light coursed out from its belly as it fell to the ground with empty eyes and an open mouth.

"I'm sorry, Adam," Mike whispered under his breath as pain started to spread all throughout his body. He saw Adam on his knees, broken and in tears. Oblivious to the light that lingered from inside the dragon.

Gradually, a figure appeared from the dragon's open mouth. It was Eve, young and beautiful like a dream. She walked over to Adam and leaned down to kiss him. She wiped away her beloved Adam's tears and extended her hand to pull him out from his body. This must be what Adam had been waiting for all his life. Mike saw Adam and Eve, hand in hand, before they vanished in a thick gust of wind.

Mike finally closed his eyes, ready to accept his death. He felt reassured knowing that Eve had been freed. His body started to convulse when he heard voices calling his name. He wanted to scream, *I'm here! I'm over here!* but nothing came out.

PART IV:
ADVENTURE AWAITS

CHAPTER TEN

- Mike -

When Mike came to, he found himself lying down in his bed in Eden as if everything had just been a bad dream. His body ached, but what hurt even more was that his father was gone.

He had no idea what happened after he passed out from the Serpent's bite. They must have found his body and brought him to the tree to get healed.

The house felt empty as Mike walked down the same steps that led to his father's study. Everything looked the same, but it felt different. *What am I going to do now*? He thought when he sat in his father's chair and wept.

After a long while of looking at Big Ben's belongings, it dawned on Mike that he wasn't the only one to grieve. He had to tell Elle about what happened to her grandparents—that's if she hadn't already heard.

Mike got ready. He wasn't entirely sure how he was going to break it to her. Before leaving, he took his Sphere and the Sword of

Wrath and flew toward Elle's house.

It was Leonard, Elle's dad, who opened the door.

"Mike," he said before hugging him. "We heard about Adam and Big Ben."

Mike nodded, trying to keep it together.

Leonard's face sank. "Your father was a good man, Mike."

"He was," Mike said sullenly. "Always did what was expected of him. About Adam and Eve. I don't know. I keep thinking, if there had been another way, would I have been able to save them?"

"We all lost a great deal," Leonard said, tears rolling down his cheek. "Two pillars have fallen in one night and as hard as it is to accept, we have to continue the fight. I'm also really concerned about Elle."

"Is Elle alright?" Mike asked.

"Well," he said, "she's trying to be. Come inside. Elle and Luna are here. They're just about to leave."

"She's leaving with Luna?" Mike asked. "Where are they heading to?"

Mike saw Emilia in the kitchen, wiping her tears with a napkin.

"Have a seat, Mike," she said before blowing her nose. "My husband and I agreed to have Luna lead her training."

"Sky Dwellers are scarce, and we've all got our hands full," Leonard said. "Luna's level of experience will greatly help our daughter to be combat-ready in no time. Three cycles to be exact."

"She'll be gone for three cycles?" he asked. "That's almost six months."

Emilia nodded, "It's for the best. If Adam trusted her, then we trust her, too."

"I see," replied Mike. "Then I'll escort her to where they're going. It's important to me that I know where to find her."

Mike heard a door open. It was Elle and Luna.

Elle didn't say anything at first, but her eyes were wet. He also noticed that she was wearing an outfit that was better fitting now that she was in Eden. She looked more like a Midian in her blue silk dress. Her hair was in a ponytail with a few strands falling down her shoulders. She was beautiful despite her sad expression. Luna also emerged from the bedroom behind her. The deer-lady tilted her head a little, making sure her antlers didn't bump the door frame. She, too, looked devastated as she tried to console Elle.

"We better get going then," Elle said.

"Elle, I'm sorry," Mike said, "I wasn't able to—"

"No," she said softly, cutting him off. "My grandparents and your father would have been proud of you," she said as her eyes started to flood.

"I won't let anything bad happen to you, Elle," Mike said with his head bowed. "My father—he wanted me to protect you. I promise, I will."

"Thank you, Mike," she replied.

Mike took her bag while Elle said her goodbyes. They soon found themselves heading north together with Willow, Kick, and Finchy.

§

Luna led the way. Behind her, Mike and Elle walked in dead silence. Even the three critters were quiet, sitting on top of the backpack on Mike's back.

At a certain point on their trek, Mike came across a familiar aftertaste of iron—of blood pumping adrenaline. There was danger hanging in the air, and it was calling to him.

"I'm sensing something," Mike said to Elle and Luna. "Stay put, I should go check it out."

He wore his Sphere and went to inspect the forest. From a distance, Mike heard the leaves rustle.

It was Jon Bulbutton, the famous capybara, frightfully scurrying across the forest. Mike took off his Sphere and dived down to grab Jon. Once he got his hands on him, they went up in the air and sped away.

"Need a lift, Sir Jon?" Mike asked as he held the furry brown capybara in his arms.

"Mike! Am I glad to see you!" Jon said. "Now quick! Take me to Luna. There's something urgent I need to tell her."

"Is everything okay?" asked Mike.

"That scheming scoundrel thought he could just hunt me down like some helpless prey," Jon said indignantly. "You won't believe what I found out, Mike. I have proof I tell you! That sun wolf—Luna's twin brother, is in fact a spy! He was the one that tipped the Serpent about our plans. The fall of Eden's pillars was his doing."

Mike's eyebrows furrowed. "If that is true, then we need to act. Fast. If there's anyone who knows how to take down that wolf, it would definitely be Luna."

Mike tried to calm himself as he came back for Elle.

When Mike landed, Jon hopped off and quickly ran toward Luna.

Luna's eyes widened as Jon told him about the sun wolf.

"Change of plans," she said. "All of you, we're going to have to travel by moon."

Right before their eyes, Luna had transcended into a noble doe. Her fur was silky brown. She had majestic antlers and a pair of beady eyes.

"Climb up and be quick," she said. "The sun is closing in. He's on our tail."

Mike lifted Jon Bulbutton and helped Elle saddle up.

"You guys go ahead," Mike said. "I'm going to stay behind and fight him off."

The deer tapped its leg demandingly. "Hop on, or we all stay."

Mike knew he wouldn't be able to fight off Luna's stubbornness. He was left with no choice but to join Elle and Jon on Luna's back.

The deer immediately sprinted forward as a streak of moonlight lit the path. The moment the moon's light caught them, the deer started to float. Mike held on tight, making sure Elle was in between his arms and wouldn't fall off. He liked how warm she felt and the smell of lavender in her hair.

Mike shook his head. What Erin had said still bothered him. *What if she was right? What if I am going soft because of her?* Mike knew that he shouldn't let himself be vulnerable. He had to be strong. Stronger than both of his parents if he had to, especially now that he was alone. But that was the thing—he didn't really want to be alone.

The next few seconds passed by in a blur. Luna had sky-rocketed them far to the north, and they soon found themselves descending slowly onto the land of flying squirrels. It was cold, and there was a dewy radiance that clouded their eyes. They were in a valley, high up in the mountains where there were Baobab tree villages, where scurries of flying squirrels lived.

Mike hopped off and helped Elle get down the deer's back.

"Thank you," Elle said.

Luna transcended into a tall regal woman with antlers that served her more like a crown. She whistled. One of the squirrels quickly came up to meet her.

"M'lady," it said, "Anything I can do for you?"

"I will need you to send a message to the elder, Umi. You will find her in Higher Gan," Luna said. "Make sure you are not followed, and deliver it yourself."

"Yes, m'lady. What message have you?" replied the squirrel.

"Do not trust the sun wolf," Luna said.

The squirrel nodded and went on its way.

They continued to walk further, traversing the village until they approached a ravine that was so high, it looked like gates to another dimension. Luna treaded the path so confidently that she hadn't looked over her shoulder even once. After passing through the ravine, they came up to a cave that had a tunnel-like passage.

"Are we really going in there?" asked Mike.

Luna nodded firmly and went in ahead of them. Mike had his guard up as they all followed her through the dark cavern. They walked through slippery moss-laden rocks. It felt like it took forever until they saw light come through at the end of the tunnel.

It was getting a lot colder now, and when they emerged from the cave, the forest before them was covered with a thick blanket of snow.

"Oh dear," muttered Jon Bulbutton. "I don't think we're at all equipped to travel in the snow."

"No need to fret," Luna said as she took out the vial that was attached to her necklace. She opened the cap and took a sip before handing it to Elle. "One drop each," she said.

Mike made sure that every one of them had their share of the liquid before he took his. Surprisingly, the drink made them feel warm all over. When Mike jumped down onto the waist-deep snow, the ice melted, splashing warm water on his feet. It was like a snow hole with a radius of about two feet. His feet were wet, but at least he wasn't shivering in the cold. They continued treading forward, leaving a streak of steamy water along their path.

"That drink is brilliant!" uttered Elle as they strolled on.

Luna smiled at her, and without a word, she transformed into a deer. She walked ahead and led them through the snow.

"Isn't it odd," Elle said to Mike. "Luna has antlers. I mean, aren't stags supposed to have them and not does?"

"Come to think of it," Mike replied, "I guess that means that if you meet a doe with antlers then you can bet that it's a Midian. Women need it for self-defense, too, of course."

Mike's legs were beginning to cramp and the effect of their drink was also starting to wear off. The two feet radius of melting snow was now just a few inches from their bodies and they were equally feeling the chill.

"Just a little more," Luna said.

They soon reached a hot spring in the middle of the snow. It was about the size of a pond with water steaming up directly on top of the moon. It was a majestic sight. The deer drew closer to the moon's reflection, and she touched the moon with the tip of her nose. As the warm ripples touched the soil, the snow vanished.

The deer shape-shifted back as Luna took out her vial and collected the water as it began to rise. The moon loomed more closely, appearing as big as a beach ball. Its nearness started to pull the gravity of the water, making the pond float like a clear, blue, water orb. Once Luna had filled up her vial, she turned to her companions and gestured with her hands to what lay behind them.

CHAPTER ELEVEN

- Elle -

Elle turned around and was awestruck to find out that they were in a different place. It was a village filled with deer folk, and it was teeming with life and festivities. Their houses were like domes. Some of them were boldly colored while others were transparent like snow globes. The snow was gone, but the soil remained pearly white, and the tree trunks were also white with yellowish leaves.

"Shall we?" asked a wide-eyed boy with newly sprung antlers on top of his ruffled chocolate-brown hair. The young deer handed them a wooden plate and impatiently escorted them to their seat.

"Oh, don't be shy," an older plump woman said. "Come and sit down."

The woman had puffed, rosy cheeks, twinkly blue eyes, curly brown hair, and roundish antlers. Her rag-like dress swooshed on her wide frame.

"I'm sure you're going to love my cooking! I'm Lady Berger.

That's my son, Pim. Come now, Pim, and help set up the table," she said as she busily laid out loaves and bowlfuls of steaming hot soup on top of a long log table.

Mike and Elle exchanged looks as they sat down. Everyone in the camp, both male and female, had the stature of a warrior except for Mrs. Berger. The tables started to fill up, and soon, Mike and Elle found themselves ducking antlers whenever a deer person would reach for the salad fork. There were laughter, drum beats, and the clanking of utensils.

Mrs. Berger jovially wrapped an arm around Elle as she poured grape juice into her cup.

"Let's celebrate, dear! It's a full moon, you see? Pretty soon, on the second full moon after the autumnal equinox, we will leave the Deer Camp and travel far, very far from here. We sure love to travel by moon."

Elle wanted to ask where it is they go to, but Mrs. Berger's attention was diverted when Luna joined their table. The thumping of the drums went silent, and everyone leaned in and paid attention to the moon deer except for Pim.

"You're a huge mouse," Pim said to Jon Bulbutton, who had just taken his seat across the table.

"Yes, child, I am a capybara," Jon said, tipping his head like a gentleman. "You can say that I'm a mouse that grew ten times over."

"Dear sir," Luna said, "would you kindly enlighten us in detail as to the trouble my brother Sunny has been causing this time?"

"That Sunny boy is just impossible to get along with!" Jon said. "I'm sure you all remember that a couple of cycles ago, Sunny fell ridiculously in love with a girl. He was like a mad dog. But the gal, well, let's say she knew better."

"Yes, I remember," Luna said with a loud sigh of disappointment.

"It was the first time that someone transcended into a tree."

"A tree?" Elle blurted out.

"Yes, dear." Jon said. "In her desire to get away from him, she willed herself so hard that she transcended into a tree."

"That time, my brother lost it," continued Luna. "He didn't eat. Didn't sleep. He didn't talk at all for a couple of days. Nevertheless, Sunny continued to love and care for this beautiful tree and even offered her the sun. She would get nourishment and feed on the light, and it gave him peace—that she will live her life forever with him."

"That was the time when he didn't cause any trouble at all," Jon said. "As if he had been out of our system while gifting us with a most wondrous sunshine. As for me, well, we all know that trees are my specialty."

"You do make the most wondrous architectural feats!" Willow said from Elle's lap.

"Why, thank you," Jon said. "Anyhow, recently, Sunny commissioned me to carve the tree into the image of the girl he loved. I thought it was a wonderful gesture, and I agreed to do it—for half a cycle in fact. But then, after I finished working on it, it started to rain so very hard! A bolt of thunder struck the tree and it split the trunk in half. It was awful!

"I tried looking everywhere for him, but he was hard to find. At one point, I just gave up and went back to the thunderstruck tree. That's when I saw Sunny. I was going to apologize for what happened, when all of a sudden, he pulled out a shard of glass. From it, I saw the Serpent, giving him false promises that he would return his lady back to her original form in exchange for information. I knew Sunny wouldn't just agree to such a thing, but his emotions had bested him. He must have been angry and confused when he saw the tree. Now, the sun wolf is targeting me because I witnessed him being a snitch."

"Jon," Luna said, dejectedly. "I'm very sorry for the distress that my brother has caused."

Jon sighed deeply. "How are we going to handle him, Luna?"

"Options are," she said, "we either set a trap for him, or knowing my brother, he'll try to get close enough to know the Grandmaster's weakness and eventually turn on him. And then, the last option would be, we do nothing and have him lead us to the Grandmaster. We'll have to weigh each option, and I will personally speak with the elders about it."

Somehow, Elle felt pity for the wolf. He must have spiraled into becoming someone he didn't want to be. But then again, Sunny didn't have to betray everybody in order to prove his devotion to the one he loved.

When the meal was over, everyone headed toward the pond that floated like a crystalline ball. Some sat in a circle around it while others danced and sang songs of bravery. Pim jumped in and sat in between her and Mike. Pretty soon, the little deer found himself being lulled to sleep by the harmonious voices of the women in their tribe as they beautifully chanted and danced in honor of the moon. Mrs. Berger spotted Pim and quickly carried him off to bed.

Jon Bulbutton, Willow, Kick, and Finchy Jr. had also joined in the merriment. They danced freely to the beat of the drums. For some reason, Elle and Mike were in their own little bubble, exchanging glances as they talked. Maybe it was because of the moon, creating an invisible pull of gravity between them. Maybe it was that or maybe it was because they had recently shared the same pain, making them feel like they needed each other to breathe.

When Mrs. Berger came back, she dragged both of them into the circle. They felt awkward at first but as the drumbeats lingered, it became harder to ignore. Pretty soon, they found themselves raising their hands and stomping their feet.

Elle peered at the globular body of water that magnified the moon. There was an image there, like a face, etched onto the moon's craters.

The drums stopped when Luna stood up with her hands spread wide.

"Ladies and Gentlemen," she said as the crowd turned their attention to her. "Land Dwellers of the Deer family, let's all give a warm welcome to Jon Bulbutton, a great visionary and friend. Also with us is Michael, the phoenix, Redeemer of Eve, son of Sir Ben Gabriel and Her Highness the Cherubim, bearer of the Sword of Wrath. And of course, Lady Uriel, the Last Mystery and the first Sky Dweller from the direct line of Adam and Eve, soon to be bearer of the Tranquil Blade."

Everybody cheered and applauded. "These two may be Sky Dwellers," Luna said, "but they shall walk among us, with us, and for us. With them, we, too, hope for peace and to continue what our friend, Adam, had started."

Luna looked at her guests. "May his soul be at rest. We offer this night to honor Adam and Ben Gabriel, our beloved pillars of Eden.

"Now, the time has come. My family would like to turn over a gift, one that our race has concealed and guarded with our lives for generations. In return, we only ask for your bravery and perseverance as you face the challenges ahead. I would like to call forth Uriel to receive one of Eve's Four Whiloms, The Tranquil Blade, the Land Dweller's Whilom."

Luna took out the sword from its mantle and raised it skyward.

Elle breathed in deeply and came forward. Before her, Luna appeared humbled as she lowered the sword.

"Your grandmother once failed to slay the Serpent with this

sword," she said as she handed over the Whilom. "The demon took her over. He took her rib and told her to eat the fruit from the Tree of Knowledge, a fruit that he had coated with malice. When I saw this happen, I knew she had been compromised, and so I took the sword from her just in time before she transformed into a dragon."

Luna looked straight into her eyes and spoke softly. "I pray that you will be able to accomplish the duties your forefathers have failed to do."

Luna then steadied her gaze firmly back to the crowd, "And now, we shall help in training Uriel for three cycles. Each cycle will have three leaders of my choosing."

The doe bowed and smiled at her. Elle wasn't quite sure what to say. Somehow, she was relieved to have all these people help figure things out with her. Inside her was a glint of hope after hearing about Eve. Her grandmother had done the best she could.

§

After the ceremony, Luna called for Mike. They were nearby and Elle was able to overhear them talking.

"I know this is sudden," the moon deer said, "but I would need a Sky Dweller to be Elle's first cycle trainer. I believe you've received the best swordsmanship training while you were under Boris Steele's apprenticeship. That makes you the perfect candidate in teaching her how to wield a sword."

"I'd be honored," Mike said. "But I can't help but think about my other duties."

"It will only be for one cycle," replied Luna, "And this duty is of great importance, don't you think?"

Mike nodded.

"Good," Luna said. "I would personally escort you out of camp when the task is done."

She gestured toward Mrs. Berger to lead the newcomers to their quarters. They were all placed in one dome. The girls were on one side, separated by a curtain from the boys.

"I apologize for the lodging," Mrs. Berger said. "We weren't quite expecting a group to arrive. Well, goodnight everyone."

She beamed at them as she padded out quietly out of the room.

On the bed, Elle inspected the Tranquil Blade. It was a ridiculously balanced long-grip sword. She held it and was pleased with the distinct markings. The one that was most noticeable was the markings of a dragon's face. It was like a logo that was traced along the bottom of the blade with a gleaming mirror-like finish. The blunt edge was matte, and the butt of the sword had intricate design.

From the other side of the room, she heard Mike's voice.

"Hey Elle," she heard him say.

Elle blinked, realizing how near his voice sounded. "Umm, hey, Mike. Can't sleep?"

"No, I don't think I can. I keep thinking about my father."

"Same. I wish I could have seen my grandmother at least once," Elle said as she laid the sword down beside her. "Mike?"

"Yeah?" he replied.

"I'm scared," Elle muttered.

"Everything will be okay."

"I can't believe I'm actually going to use a sword. Will you really train me?" she asked.

"I will. That sword was meant for you."

"Meant for me?"

"It is. How about I tell you more about where that sword came from?"

"I'd like that." she replied.

"You see, when I was six years old, my dad entrusted me to Sir Boris Steele. I became his apprentice. This man, Boris, belonged to a rhino family, known for their craft as the best bladesmiths—they are the ones who created these Whiloms. Boris, on the other hand, did more than that. He tested each sword he made. That gave him the reputation as the best swordsman of all time. He's rather old now, but either way, he's still as fierce and burly as ever."

Elle listened intently. For some reason, the sound of Mike's voice was very calming. She also imagined what Mike would have looked like when he was six years old. How adorable he must have been.

"He was my mentor," Mike said. "He was the one who taught me how to duel and forge weapons. I remember that one day, after we had finished a set, Sir Boris asked me to sit with him along the front steps of the shop. We watched passersby and traders scuttle along the alley. Then he told me that my mother had also been his apprentice when she was younger, like me."

"Oh. He knew your mother too?" Elle asked.

"He did. He also told me one of his family's greatest secrets. It was a bit amusing, because there we were, talking casually about this huge secret, but no one in the alley cared to listen nor eavesdrop."

"A secret? Did he tell you?"

"He told me that his family had made a sword that was as equally special as the Sword of Wrath. That the alloy used in making these weapons came from a mineral taken from both the sun and the moon, and they are famed for being so rare. They were the hardest and the lightest of minerals ever to be encountered. It is also well known that the moon's mineral was so lightweight that it weighed almost as light as a feather, whereas the sun mineral was too rigid and stubborn to begin with. It required everyone in their rhino family to forge it because they had to take turns hammering. It endured exactly ten thousand strikes and likewise broke a couple of their best hammers. The composition of the Sword of Wrath had more sun mineral mixed in its alloy, while the other sword had more of the moon's mineral. There had been no use for such weapons at that time, and it was the Creator that had revealed to him their purpose. The first one, the Sword of Wrath, was meant for Punishment, whereas the second one, the Tranquil Blade, was for Mercy."

Elle gasped. She sat up in bed and looked at the Tranquil Blade. *That dragon emblem, I've seen it before*. Elle remembered her grandfather's journal and took it out.

"Mike, I need you to check something out for me. This emblem is also on the Whilom. Does it mean anything?" she asked.

Along the headrest where the edge of the curtain was, Elle slipped the journal to Mike's side of the room.

"This belonged to my grandfather. But I can't understand anything written on it."

Mike took the book and gently opened it.

"It could be a marking to distinguish Eve's four Whiloms. You see, as a dragon, Eve was able to acquire all four, given that she was a unique one. She was a creature that had belonged to all four Midian races. She was a Sky Dweller, a Land Dweller, a Sea Dweller, and a Wanderer. Right now, you have her Land Dweller Whilom. You still need to acquire the rest."

Elle heard him flip through the pages.

"Would you want me to translate this for you?" he asked.

"Only if it's okay with you."

"It's no problem at all."

"Thanks, Mike. It would mean so much to me," Elle said. "Well, we should be up early for training tomorrow. I guess this is goodnight."

"Yeah, we had a long journey. Goodnight Elle," she heard him say.

Since that night, Mike would read to her from behind the curtain. Because of this, Elle often looked forward to bed. She liked how there would be times when they would just talk to each other.

She found that little by little with each passing day, she would open up to him a whole lot more.

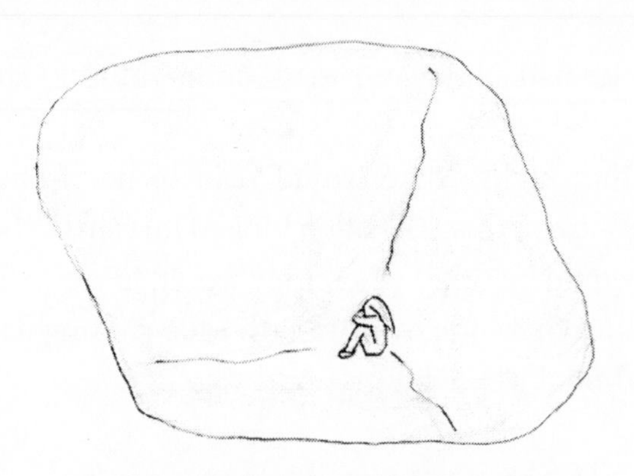

CHAPTER TWELVE

- Mike -

When morning came, drumbeats resounded in the village, waking Midians from their slumber. Mike walked out of the dome and saw Pim wave at him.

"Good morning, Mike!"

"Good morning, Pim! Do you know where Luna is?"

"Oh, she's waiting for you by the water orb. Elle is on her way there, too," replied Pim.

As Mike walked briskly, he was able to pass by a couple of deer people coming in from the fields with baskets of fresh produce. Everyone seemed busy. Some were sharpening their weapons, making clay pots, and hanging up clothes.

"Elle!" Mike exclaimed when he caught up with her, but oddly, all he got was an anxious smile.

"Nervous?" he asked.

"Yeah. I was just thinking about Hillworth. Can you believe it? Just a few days ago, I was concerned about grades on paper. But now, I might actually doom everybody."

"Good morning Sky Dwellers," Luna said as she greeted them.

“Today, we start training, and Elle, just to be clear, you’ll need to learn quickly if you are to save mankind and bring back the balance.”

Elle winced. “Is it really necessary? Fighting, I mean.”

“To fight with honor, yes,” she replied. “That is what we’ll teach you for three cycles.

“Every day after breakfast, you will undergo two hours of Introductory Lessons. I will personally teach you about Eden, the multitude of worlds, and the creatures in it. You will know more about the strengths and weaknesses of the Wanderers in order to create the proper strategies.”

Mike watched Elle nod as Luna detailed the rest of the program.

“After your lunch break, you will then undergo three hours of Physical Strength Training to be taught by Mike. It’s mainly comprised of endurance, core power, and combat training. You’ll be tired after that so you should get a bit of rest.

“Lastly, after supper, you must head to the topmost tier of the village for one hour of Spiritual Awakening. The program will be taught by Master Queti, an elder deer. He will teach you how to focus your energy and find your inner strength. It is aimed at reinforcing your sense of duty while also teaching you how to harness certain powers that you have yet to unlock. Most of all, it will provide you with exercises on how to block outside forces that may try to control you, like that of the Serpent. Finishing this program is crucial. Hopefully, you get to transcend before the three cycles end.”

“Alright,” Elle said. “I’ll do my best.”

“Good. Get some breakfast, and then we begin.”

§

Mike planned out his training course while Elle had her morning session with Luna. He had to take extra precaution with the program because Elle hadn't transcended yet. He needed to tailor-fit his methods based on what she was capable of.

Once he had prepped everything, he decided to take his lunch a little earlier than everybody else.

Mike was enjoying the last bite of his sandwich when Elle emerged.

"Mike! There you are!" she exclaimed.

Mike waved back. "Hey! I'm actually done," he said, pointing at his empty plate. "I'll wait for you by the trail, okay? Better not eat too heavy or you'll puke," he said grinning.

"Yeah, yeah," Elle replied with a light-hearted laugh. "Between the two of us, I'm pretty sure you'll give up on me once you realize how much I suck at fighting."

Mike had to smile as Willow, Kick, and Finchy surrounded Elle and greeted her excitedly. He really liked seeing her this happy.

Near the trail, Mike was able to spot some of the deer folk as they wrapped up their morning exercises. He was reading the obstacle course that spanned just as long as the trail when one of them, a brusque man, came up to him with his chest out and his head held high. Mike also noticed a yellowish fruit wedged on his antler. "Taking on the course are we?" he asked.

"Yeah, I guess," Mike replied.

"Oi, just so you know—First-timers shouldn't complete it in one run. It's gonna kill ya' if you're not careful. Just get the hang of it for now, yeah?"

"Okay. Thanks for the tip," he said, trying not to sound arrogant.

"No sweat. Now I'm off to stuff my face with Mrs. Berger's

wonderful cooking," he said as he slid off the pear-like fruit from his antler and threw it in his direction before eagerly walking away.

Mike caught it, rubbed it on his chest, and took a bite. He had an hour to himself. Might as well warm up.

Amid the warning, he knew he'd still go for it. He should be able to make it anyway. Mike found himself loving the entire course. The Land Dwellers really do take their trainings seriously. It had a lot of hidden traps that were extra challenging.

Elle was warming up by the time Mike got back to the starting line. She was able to watch him run the final stretch, but she kept flinching after he almost got hit by a swaying log.

He did it! Mike felt so exhilarated in completing the course that he ended up lifting Elle in the air.

"Whoa there, tiger!" Elle exclaimed, her cheeks blushing.

"Oh! My bad," Mike said as he took her down. "Tiger? Really, Elle?"

She shook her head jokingly. "Sorry, it just came out of my mouth. Next time it's going to be 'whoa, phoenix' for sure."

"Great. Now it's time for you to do all four courses!" he said with a wide grin. "Just kidding! First, we need to work on cardio. That means you've got to finish the trail run."

"Okay," she replied as she went into a sprint position along the starting line.

"Alright, I'm going to record your time so that we get to see your progress," he said. "Ready in three, two, one, go!"

Elle dashed as fast as she could. The instant she turned a corner, Mike quickly wore his Sphere, making him invisible as he flew up and watched over Elle. What she didn't know was that Mike had set a trap in the middle of the trail. For him, this was the real test. He wanted to see how she was going to deal with frustration, helplessness, and failure.

Mike was oblivious at first, but it was a test on himself too.

For some reason, he felt jittery when Elle crashed down and was trapped inside the hole. It was hard to ignore her cries for help as she tried her best to climb out. The urge to save her started to well up inside of him. *No. I'm her teacher. I can't pull her out just yet.* But when Elle actually started to cry, Mike felt awful. He was going to have to live with the fact that he was the one that broke her spirit. She at least deserved a few more minutes to redeem herself and learn to overcome this. Mike watched as Elle stood back up and wiped her tear-stained cheeks.

She took a moment, and under her breath, Mike heard her mention her grandfather's name. And somehow, with renewed strength, Elle was able to climb out of the hole. She had carved out footholds onto the side of the pit and lifted herself free. For a few seconds, she laughed as she lay on the ground. She then stood up, dusted herself off, and continued to sprint.

Mike watched her in deep admiration as she reached the finish line.

"Oh man!" Elle said as she tried to catch her breath, "I fell in this huge pit along the trail. But I'm okay, really."

"You sure?" Mike replied.

"Yeah, I'm sure. It shouldn't be there though. Anyway, what's next?"

"I guess I could start teaching you about different types of weapons and how to dodge them," Mike replied.

He knew this skill would come in handy for her since she hadn't unlocked her powers yet. Defense first and attack only when necessary.

They rested under the shade of a tree shortly after training.

"Thanks for agreeing to train me, Mike," Elle said.

"Sure thing, no need to thank me," he replied.

"At least I didn't puke. That should be record-breaking, right?" Elle said with a laugh. "Well, I better go freshen up for supper. I guess I'll catch you in a bit. This schedule Luna gave is pretty grueling," she said as she stood up and left.

Mike felt beat. He had a good long bath and had supper too. The food was wonderful. They had potato salad, leek pasta, and banana pudding. Mike was a little surprised—he knew Land Dwellers were a proud race, but he also found it hard to ignore how warm they were. The deer folk had made him feel as if he was a part of their family even though he was a Sky Dweller.

It was too overwhelming that he had to excuse himself. Mike missed his father terribly and there was no one else he could talk to about it. Elle would still be with Master Queti and won't be back until later.

Alone in the room, Mike ended up working on translating Adam's journal. Whenever he read things about his father, he would pause, allowing it to sink in. He was gone now. He had no family left. After a while, his mind would wander to the home that no longer felt like home.

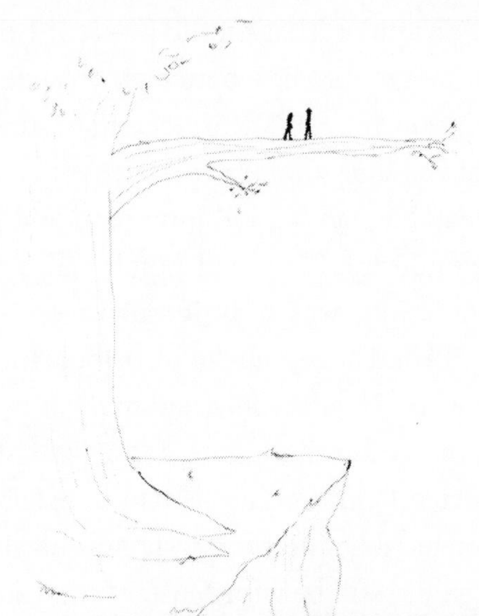

CHAPTER THIRTEEN

- Elle -

Elle was at her desk first thing after breakfast. Her gaze wandered to the photos that were hanging on the walls inside the green dome. They showed the different transformations of the four Midian races—centaurs, griffins, manatees, and serpents. She was looking at them closely when Luna's voice came out of nowhere, startling her.

"Good morning, Elle," Luna said.

She was standing by the door, looking at her with a set of grey eyes that may have seen everything there was to see in the world. "Would you like to enumerate the duties of each Midian race based on what we've discussed yesterday?"

Elle sat straight behind her desk. "Yes, ma'am," she said. "Sky Dwellers, the winged creatures, are the guardians and promoters of peace and unity. They are given the task to help and assist mankind in fulfilling a promise. Le-Ovedah, that man should preserve and look after their world."

"Correct," Luna said. "But of course, since the population of Sky Dwellers has dropped at an alarming rate, we are now facing a huge imbalance. They were supposed to be man's guardians, but it would seem that they are in fact becoming endangered themselves."

Elle blinked. *Maybe there were others like her—Sky Dwellers who haven't been able to transcend.*

"Alright. Please proceed," Luna said, nodding in her direction.

Elle cleared her throat and continued. "Land Dwellers, creatures born with great strength. They are our heroes, noble and brave. They protect the land and keep it bountiful."

"Good," replied Luna. "Now, onto the next one."

"Sea Dwellers," Elle went on saying. "They are the protectors of the seas. They have the power to control the tides. Some are masters of illusion while others have psychic abilities. These beings are said to be highly inclined to art."

Luna nodded and sat on her desk. "Ah, Sea Dwellers. It is best to also be wary of them. They can be very peculiar and mysterious. Most of them have a tendency to be fickle and emotional, even to the extent wherein they desire to be admired and uphold beauty and image above all else. Sometimes you won't see them for who or what they really are because they are very guarded creatures."

Elle thought about her mom. She remembered instances wherein she had chosen beauty over practicality. Fame over meaningful relationships. Vanity over purpose. It was vanity that made her an actress. It was also vanity that made her stop, more specifically, because of wrinkles.

"Luna?" Elle called out. "What about the duties of Wanderers?" It was something they hadn't discussed yet, and she felt compelled to know the answer.

"Good question," replied Luna as she stood near the picture

of a crocodile. "There was no such thing as Wanderers back then. Reptiles were a part of the three before they broke away."

"I see," Elle nodded firmly. "Also, I have a question."

"What is it?"

"These planets above Eden, are they inhabited?"

"Yes. Eden is the station that has access to all the worlds."

"So," Elle said. "Are you saying that Eden is like a halfway house and that there are numerous societies out there?"

"Why wouldn't there be? Of course, there are others besides Earth," she replied.

"Okay. Oh! I have another question again," Elle blurted out. "I've been hearing things about the wolf, Sunny."

Luna didn't reply, but she did give her a cryptic look.

"I mean, he's your brother, and I just find it surprising how different you are compared to him," Elle explained.

Luna leaned against the table.

"It's actually very simple. My brother chose a different path. Or perhaps it was I who chose a different path," she said, her eyebrows furrowed, thinking deeply. "He takes short cuts, and I do not. Even though we're both gifted, I see that his powers are also the source of his weakness. Life seemed easy for him. Too predictable. Too boring. But he is still my brother. He's not perfect, but then again, who is? What standards do we have for perfection? Personally, I do not believe in perfection. It's only a figment of man's imagination. Life as we know it—came from the Creator's furnace—an explosion in the heavens."

Elle nodded, trying to grasp the context of what she was saying.

"Believe it or not," Luna continued. "Sunny did try to achieve perfection in his own way, yet there is this one flaw. He never believed in anything other than himself. Never had anything worthy to live and die for up until he met that girl. But I guess it was all too late. I have reason to believe that this girl was used as a tool to get my brother into doing the Serpent's bidding."

"So, he works for him now?" Elle asked.

"He will work for him for a while, yes, but only to find a way to outsmart him. If given the chance, he will find the best shortcut he can get and redeem himself. I know my brother because I was like him once. That means he could still change. The girl he loved would have been the key, but she's gone now," Luna said.

"I can't imagine you ever being like him," Elle said.

Luna gave a small approving laugh. "That's alright, it was a long time ago anyway. Back when Sunny and I were kids, we had to learn archery. Our tradition was that during the eclipse, he and I should duel and see who was the better warrior. That said, if you see an eclipse happen anytime soon, it means that he and I are going to face each other and fight. Back then, I remember how I hated losing, so I decided to take a shortcut by cutting off both my breasts in order to gain a better stance and posture when holding up my bow. And yes, this decision made me win against my brother. I felt powerful and proud. I was arrogant, thinking that I knew better. But that was until I met the great ape."

"Adam?" Elle's eyes flung wide open.

"Yes, Adam. We met outside of Eden. He wanted to take the sword which I had taken from Eve. I refused, of course, but I underestimated him. When he saw my wounds, he told me that I had already lost. I lost the moment I decided to alter who I was. That I had gained nothing. Then he invited me into his home."

"And then, what happened?" asked Elle.

"At first, I thought it odd, but soon enough we became friends and his wisdom grew on me like a seed, and this, my brother could never have. He may have the sun's power but I have the wisdom of the moon."

Elle knew exactly what she meant. Her grandpa always had his way of making people see things from a different perspective.

"After talking with Adam," Luna said, "he decided to leave the sword with me and asked that I vow to protect it and ensure that it does not fall into the wrong hands."

"Yeah, that sounds exactly like him. Oh man, you should have seen him in court," Elle said with a hint of a smile on her face. Discernment was in fact one of his most commendable gifts. *Maybe that's why grandpa had continued to believe that Eve had been innocent for so long.*

"You see that water orb over there?" Luna pointed at the open window. "Most of the time I would look at my reflection in it and what I would see was the face of my brother pasted on mine. Our reflections are so alike. I hated it. It reminded me of who I used to be. But it was this that made me realize that I do not hold the same standards as I did before."

Elle smiled, knowing that her grandfather had influenced so many lives, including Luna's.

"If you believe that Sunny can change," Elle said. "I'll help you. I don't know how I'll do it since I haven't even transcended yet, but I'll do my best."

"Thank you," Luna said. "Le-Ovedah."

"Well, I also have a couple of questions about transcending."

"Ah! Yes, of course," Luna replied. "Knowledge is the key, but oftentimes, knowledge hides in the shadows."

Elle wanted to ask her what she had meant, but Luna had already started talking about the different kinds of Wanderers, which was, of course, greatly interesting.

She enjoyed Luna's lectures. As her teacher, Luna didn't just dump information at her. Luna was actually teaching her something that was a lot more vital. Elle couldn't quite pinpoint it, but it was there, as if Luna was teaching her the process of *how* to think, instead of *what* to think.

§

Elle walked out of the dome and found Pim laughing and running amok as he played tag with his friends. He ran to Mrs. Berger and drew her skirt up like a shield. Willow, Kick, and Finchy were also in on the fun as the three critters clung onto Mrs. Berger's antlers.

"Oh! You rotten deerlings. Take this and place it on the table," she said handing them some food trays. The children looked miserable now that they had to stall playing to help out.

Jon Bulbutton also appeared to have been busy. He dusted his arms as he walked toward the lunch table. "How's the statue coming along, Sir Jon?" Elle asked as the capybara drew near.

"Oh, it's the least I could do for Luna. Because of the sheer size of it, as well as my lack of tools, I'd say I might have it done by the time of the equinox, give or take."

Jon raised his head upward when a shadow passed across the table. Flying above them was Mike. He landed near the table and gave Elle a wry smile.

Elle said with a smirk, "So, what surprise do you have for me now? I reckon it's something that will try to kill me."

"Something like that, yes," Mike said jokingly as he sat down and placed some salad on his plate.

The lunch tables were rapidly becoming occupied, and chatter resounded as usual, but Elle didn't hear any of it. Her mind was busy thinking about what Luna had said earlier. She wondered about the standards of perfection. What is it that most people often expect?

Of course, it's always easy to doubt the Creator for allowing bad things to happen, and there are questions as to why bad people even exist. It's all about *why, why, why…*

Elle was so deep in contemplation that she had forgotten the salad on her plate. The answer, she thought, could be Free Will. She tried to imagine life without it and realized that life without Free Will was quite depressing. The Creator would have been some kind of dictator who controlled people's thoughts and actions. Better yet, it would be as if the Creator made robots as opposed to thinking human beings.

If what we wanted was to experience genuine happiness, then we would need to have Free Will to do so. The Creator cannot order a person to be happy like a jester in a circus. Instead, He must have chosen the good with the bad and everything else in between. It was the price He had to pay to give mankind the fighting chance to find happiness. He must have seen true perfection in it, one that wasn't merely a picture-perfect rip-off. A fake. A fraud.

§

After having lunch, Elle suited up and prepared for her next training. She tied her hair up and latched the Tranquil Blade to her left side and a leather belt bag to the other. She closed her eyes and breathed in deep as she pictured herself as a warrior—a Sky Dweller. Her entire body was still aching from yesterday's training, but it felt good. It was the kind of pain that made her feel stronger.

She walked past the obstacle course and further toward the Warrior's Terrain, a forest area that was cordoned off.

"There you are," Mike said when he caught sight of her. "Ready to take things up a notch?"

Elle snickered. "That depends. Do I even have a choice?"

Mike walked up to her and lifted her by the waist. He flew her up on top of a tree that hung sideways off a cliff.

"For today, we're going to work on your balance and have you move confidently from great heights," he said. "All you need to do is to mimic my movements."

"Alright," Elle replied while shifting her weight slowly to test the integrity of the tree from under her feet.

Mike turned around and walked toward the very edge, and Elle followed slowly behind, feeling like a pirate's captive who was being made to walk the plank. *This shouldn't be hard*, she thought, but her body betrayed her. Her mouth went dry, her heart started to pound against her chest, and her knees grew soft like Jell-O so that she had to sit down. Looking down at the cliff below made her stomach turn, and she had to grip tightly onto the bark of the tree. She had no safety net. She had no Aeris who could make her momentarily fly. She could actually die.

"Breathe, Elle," she heard Mike say, but it sounded like an echo from far away and her vision swayed and narrowed as if she was in a blurry dream.

Elle closed her eyes. All she was able to hear clearly was the pounding fear in her heart.

"Grandpa," she cried out like a six-year-old who had tripped and fallen onto the pavement. She imagined her grandfather. His soft kind eyes, telling her, "Stand up. Stand up, Elle. Don't be afraid. Remember what I told you about becoming your truest self? It's when everything you used to be afraid of no longer means as much to you as the idea you hold in your heart."

Elle stayed down, feeling the rough texture of the tree against her palms, the whistling wind blowing her hair, and the warmth of the sun on her skin. She imagined looking at herself from outside her own body.

She was Elle, and just like the books she had read, she, too, was the hero of her own story.

Just breathe, she told herself while focusing her eyes on a mushroom that was growing on the side of the tree. *Sky Dwellers must be strong.*

Elle could hear Mike's voice again. "Just look straight toward me. I know you can do it."

There was something genuine in Mike's gaze that helped Elle calm down and trust in him. He wouldn't let her fall.

Elle lifted herself up and imagined herself in a playground, on a jungle gym back at Hillworth. "*Where's your sense of adventure?*" she thought, her face breaking into a grin. Suddenly, she found herself walking, making sure her footing was right. To finish the task, she quite literally just had to take one step at a time.

Mike had his hand outstretched, and she grabbed it without hesitation.

"Good, you did it!" he said. "Ready to do it again?"

Elle blinked. "You mean, we're going to walk back and forth?"

"Yes. And we'll also do some exercises until you get used to being at this height. After we finish today, you'll be running around like a natural Sky Dweller."

"Well, okay," Elle replied. She mimicked Mike as he did foot shifts and hops and certain poses while standing on one foot.

After a while, Mike started humming. It was like they were dancing to the tune. Elle smiled. She picked up the melody and hummed with him. She was actually starting to have fun and for some reason, she found herself glancing back at Mike.

Skip.

Slide.

Turn.

Hop.

Pose.

Repeat.

They started doing it faster, and whenever Elle's balance was off, Mike's hand would always be there, ready to assist her.

Elle felt good that she was able to overcome that crippling feeling of fear and having Mike there really helped her. "Thank you, Mike," she said.

"You did great," he replied. "Although, the challenges will get harder from here on out. But I'll be here."

Elle blinked, realizing that she was going to have to face new challenges on a daily basis and maybe discover new types of fear that she had yet to experience.

§

Back in the dome, Elle flopped onto the bed, the melody of Mike's humming still playing in her head and lulling her to sleep. She dreamed about her grandpa buying her ice cream after she had fallen off her bike and skinned her knee. In the dream, they sat on a curb by the park and he sang to her. At first, it was in the tune of Mike's humming, but it gradually changed into the same old song that her grandpa had always loved.

Elle woke up from her nap. She took a shower, got dressed, and went out. Her days felt long, but she had gotten used to it.

The moon was shining and the foliage surrounding them glowed bright as they all had their supper. Some of the villagers would retire to their quarters after eating while others would stay by the bonfire to listen to the most glorious songs.

Elle washed her plate and found Mrs. Berger clearing out the table.

"The meal was great, Mrs. Berger!" Elle said.

"I'm glad to hear it, dear," replied Mrs. Berger. "Now where is that silly boy?" she glanced underneath the tables. "Pim!" she called out. "Oh! I tell you, he's been a lot more cunning when it comes to dodging responsibility. Tell him I'm looking for him when you bump into the little mongrel."

"I will," Elle said before climbing solemnly up the highest part of the village.

The glass dome was like a snow globe, but instead of seeing specks of snow, she saw fireflies in it. In the dim room were pots of flowers that glowed pale blue, and the fireflies blinked warm amber around it. At the center was her spiritual teacher, a nearly blind elder deer named Master Queti. She looked at him and wondered how he had gotten his anters so worn-out that it appeared to be broken in a few parts.

Master Queti taught her numerous invocations, some meditational exercises, and certain body movements that were meant to help focus her energy or chi. The experience deepened her self-awareness, making her feel more at home in her own skin. Elle thought about how badly she wanted to become a Sky Dweller. She wanted to unlock that door inside of her so she could soar and be free to fly beside Mike and the others.

"You are distracted again, Lady Uriel," Master Queti said.

"Sorry," Elle said. "Umm, Master. You know, I think you'd make an awesome shrink if you lived in my world. Really help a lot of people and make a difference."

"And what makes you think I haven't?" replied her teacher. "We deer folk have travelled great distances across the galaxies. I have shared my gift to those in need of my good senses. Like a reindeer giving good tidings, yes?" He then laughed boisterously, knowing how people from her world perceived deer people who travel by moon.

"Alright, run along now," Master Queti said when their session ended. "This old reindeer needs rest."

Elle bowed her head as a sign of respect and left for their quarters.

She felt good knowing that she was making progress, and before falling asleep, she remembered that today was Paige's birthday. Her bestfriend must be so mad at her right now. If only there was a way she could reach her and let her know everything that's been going on.

CHAPTER FOURTEEN

- Mike -

Mike browsed through Elle's record book and noticed some improvements. Her sprint had spanned longer, her swing struck deeper, and her confidence grew fiercer in sync with her instincts.

Tomorrow marks the start of the Second Cycle—the same day he was meant to leave the deer camp. He woudn't be seeing Elle for a while, and the idea didn't sit well with him.

Kick was still fast asleep and was making cricket sounds in his corner of the room when Elle came in.

Mike cleared his throat. "Elle?" he called out.

"Yes, Mike?"

"May I come in?"

"Yeah, I guess. Is everything okay?" she asked.

"Everything's fine," he said as he pulled the curtain sideways and entered her side of the room. In his hand was the translated manuscript that he had been working on. "I wanted to give you this. I know how much your grandfather meant to you. And now, you'll be able to read it and carry a little piece of him with you."

Elle had that heartwarming expression on her face, something he would definitely always remember. She took the manuscript and held it tightly in her hands. She read some of the passages until her eyes welled up with tears. "Thank you, Mike."

"It has been an honor being of service to you," he replied.

"No, no. You're saying goodbye, aren't you?" she asked.

Mike couldn't answer her straight. "I wish I could stay longer," he said, "but the other Sky Dwellers need me to lead. I'm really going to miss having you around."

Elle extended her arms and embraced him, "Can we at least sit down and talk a little more? Without a stupid curtain between us this time."

She went over to sit on her bed and Mike bent down and sat on the floor beside her.

"You know," Elle whispered. "I'm going to miss hearing your voice before I go to sleep." She slid down on the floor beside him and rested her head on his shoulder.

It took a while for Mike to muster the courage to reach out and hold her hand. "I'm glad Luna chose me to train you."

"Me too," she replied.

"You know, as a phoenix, I've been conditioned and made aware of everybody's expectations of me. Sometimes I feel as if I am not allowed to explore my own path other than what has already been set." Mike felt her hand squeeze his.

"To be honest, I don't think I'm in the position to ask anything from anyone," he continued saying. "Elle, I don't know if you feel the same way about me, but I want you to know that I will always care about you. If there's one thing I want above all. It's knowing you'll be safe. That's more than enough for me. I won't always be there, and I fear…I fear—"

Elle's hand touched his lips, shushing him.

"I care about you too," she said softly, "I want to be there for you the same way that you're there for me. I can't really figure out what this feeling is. I wish I knew. All I know is that I feel strongly for you too."

Mike's head was swimming and his heart was shouting for joy. It was going to drive him crazy knowing he'll be thinking about her while he's away.

No longer aware of his surroundings, he held her gaze and for the first time, they kissed.

§

Mike watched how easily a well-built warrior had taken over his place. He stiffened when the new teacher touched Elle's arm as she held up a bow and arrow.

Kick gave him a pitiful look and hopped on top of his shoulder.

"So," Kick said, "how is it like leaving our Lady Uriel to this man here?"

Mike didn't answer. Instead, he asked Kick for a favor.

"Watch over her for me."

Without even waiting for an answer, Mike walked away, and didn't look back.

Elle excused herself and was able to catch up with Mike by the water orb. Luna was already there, waiting for him.

"Not going to say goodbye?" he heard her say. Mike breathed in deep before looking at her. He couldn't help it. He badly wanted to kiss her again. Maybe he would. Soon. When the time was right. He would hold her in his arms and kiss her.

"No," he answered, "just the words, take care."

Elle hugged him tightly. "Take care."

"You'll do great Elle," he said. "I believe in you."

Mike let her go. He didn't want to keep Luna waiting.

"Oh, and Elle," he said, "bear in mind that our swords are equally matched. So, take it easy on the new guy. I'm pretty sure you will break whatever weapon he's going to use on you."

"Thank you, Mike. Thank you for teaching me."

"Well, I didn't really have much of a choice, did I?" he asked jokingly with a comical frown.

"Very funny," she said, while punching him in the arm. "Although," she mumbled, her face now full of concern, "are you going to be assigned to watch over someone else?"

"It's possible they'll assign my duties during the Feast of the Guardians," replied Mike. "It's going to be held in Higher Gan."

Luna cleared her throat and walked up to them.

"Sadly," she said, "Elle won't be able to attend the feast because her training will not have been completed by then."

"I know. I really wish you could, though," he said loudly, making sure Luna was able to hear him.

"I wish I could, too," Elle said. "And I hope we meet again soon."

Luna walked in between them and held Elle's shoulder. "I'll be back by the Third Cycle," said Luna. "Rest assured that everything has been taken care of while I'm away."

Mike smiled and nodded at Elle before following behind Luna as she leaped into the water orb and disappeared.

§

Mike had been away from central Eden for quite some time, and he was sure that the elders would want him to report to them, but they were going to have to wait. There were other things he needed to do before he flew over to Higher Gan.

First, he had to pay a visit to his mentor, Boris Steele.

Second, he needed to have a talk with the Tree of Life.

Third, he wanted to check on his friends, Amos and Erin for updates. When all that is done, he would go meet the elders.

Luna, on the other hand, also had business in Bulbutton Square, which was exactly where Boris' shop was located. So, they both traveled to where most of the Land Dwellers have their residence.

The air was noticeably warmer the further they went south. Bulbutton Square was pretty easy to locate. It was surrounded by hills, and of course, there was the huge statue of Jon Bulbutton, the capybara.

"This is where I take my leave," Luna said as they landed by the statue.

"Thank you, Luna," he said. "Le-Ovedah."

Mike saw her walk away until a bunch of children flocked toward her. One gave Luna a flower and another held her hand. They all absolutely adored her.

Mike just had to smile before walking down a different lane where he could hear the heartbeat of the marketplace pumping life into its arteries and alleyways. There was the rumbling of wheelbarrows against the cobblestoned streets, and above him, orange leaves fell where little raccoons played along the treetops. Mike continued his pace and was able to catch a glimpse of the

Land Dweller's warm smiles from inside their shops and smell the invigorating scents of spices and fresh produce.

Mike turned left onto Steele alley where he found the tree he was looking for. Under it was a door with an iron plate that read, *Steele Masons*.

He knocked three times before entering the shop. Inside he saw his mentor placing an axe back into its display case. He glanced at Mike and smiled sheepishly. Boris Steele had a huge nose, a thick grey mustache, and a shiny bald head. He was wearing his usual work clothes, a soot-stained shirt and a pair of loose trousers.

"Mike? Oh, my boy! How are ye?"

"I'm coping well," Mike replied, "considering everything that's been going on."

"Come ere. Have a seat," Boris said, pointing to an anvil.

Mike sat on it and glanced at the rest of the weapons on display. "I just wanted you to know that the Tranquil Blade—the one made by your family—is now with Elle, Adam's granddaughter."

"Is that so?" replied Boris. "Are ye sure that's all ye came ere for?"

"Well, I don't really know. My father's gone, Boris," Mike said, his eyes trained steadily on the floor.

"Mike. Do ye know why Land Dwellers are the best trainers?" his mentor said. "Why do ye think yer dad sent ye to me?"

"Because you're the best swordsman there is," Mike replied.

"Exactly," Boris said. "But it's one huge mistake. Ye want to know why?"

Mike looked at him incredulously.

Boris took up his hammer and without waiting for an answer, he said, "It's because Sky Dwellers are innately peaceful creatures. Ye may be the guardians, but ye'll never be warriors like us. Ye wanted to keep the balance, so ye all rolled with it! But take a look around ye? Where is that balance now?"

Mike stood up abruptly. "Okay. So, let's say you're right. Maybe it's not about light versus dark. If so, then what? What exactly are we facing?"

Boris slammed his hammer onto an anvil with such force that it cracked.

"Yer in over yer head, kid," he said, pointing his hammer towards Mike. "Always volunteering yerselves in the frontline is what always gets ye killed!"

"We do what we can, Boris," Mike said as he walked toward the door. "I wish all Land Dwellers did the same."

He left the shop with a heavy heart. He knew that Boris must have had enough. He had trained his mother and look where it got her. And now it was his turn.

Mike sat on a curb as questions started to linger.

Was I wrong? Have we been looking at things from the wrong angle?

How are Sky Dwellers supposed to fight?

Will I also die in vain?

What's going to happen to Elle?

He remembered his father standing on top of the rooftop, looking over Hillworth.

"Be brave son. Be loving. Be good."

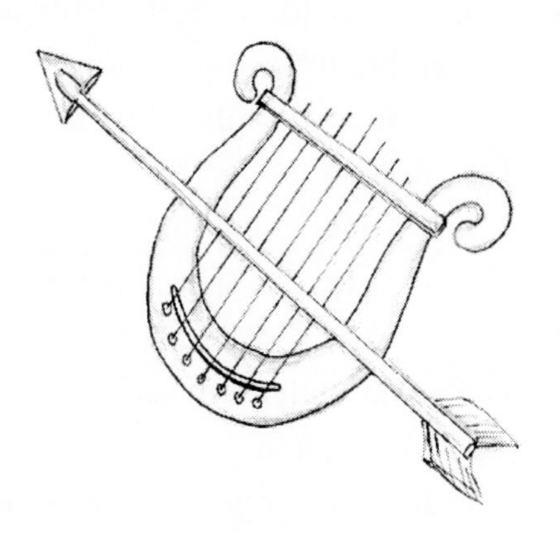

CHAPTER FIFTEEN

- Elle -

Jon Bulbutton was on top of a ladder as he worked on carving out a statue of Luna. "Hey deary," he said when he saw Elle pass by. "Can you help me reach that chisel?"

"This one?" Elle asked as she took one and handed it over to him.

"So how was your training?" Jon asked. "I see you've developed a beautiful physique. You'd be a nice subject for my next project."

"You really think so?" Elle replied. "Well, the Second Cycle is actually over. I think my trainings just keep stretching my capacity like rubber band. It's like my teachers never fail to think up new ways to further push the envelope. So far, I've had to visualize each task in great detail before actually performing anything."

"Well, it'll be over before you know it." Jon replied. "I'm sure all your hard work will pay off sooner or later."

"Thanks," she said. "I've met some of my Third Cycle teachers this morning. I hope my Spiritual Awakening coach would be easy to get along with. I'm about to meet him after supper."

"I see. How about we get some food? I sure am famished," he said as they walked together toward the dinner table.

"Is something bothering you Elle?" Jon asked.

"Oh it's nothing. I'm fine."

"You probably miss Mike."

Elle blinked, "Yeah. I do, but there's really nothing to worry about."

"Alright. You can always talk to me about anything, okay?"

"Thanks, Sir Jon," Elle replied.

Elle didn't have much of an appetite as she thought about Mike and the lessons she has learned from her classes.

Being here in Eden has given her a strong sense of purpose. Although she did have to deal with certain expectations, she was well aware that they were expectations of vital consequences. She somehow felt liberated as she thought about her world. Back there, it was as if everyone were inside hamster cages of their own creation. She felt quite detached from it now. No more daily feeds about cats doing silly things or fake news. She was free from the bombardment of worldly noise. Noise that often drowned people to a point wherein they lose or question their own value and sense of self. The idea made her think about how her dad often misplaced his car keys—what do you do when you lose that tiny little thing you need to drive and get somewhere?

Elle gazed at the deer people sitting at the dinner table. Back at Hillworth, she had always felt like an outsider looking in—like a ghost who didn't really belong anywhere. But there was something about being surrounded by Midians that meant a great deal to her. Being around them made her reconnect with life in general, and for that, she was eternally grateful.

They may have the skills and all the resources at their disposal, but they chose a life that was slow-paced. One wherein they could literally stop and smell the flowers and even have enough time to let love bloom. Take Pim for example, this little dude who could actually go out and play and be a real ki—

"Hey! Give that back!" shouted Pim.

Pim was on Elle's lap, and she noticed that he, too, had grown a little.

"Hey, your antlers are starting to develop," she told him.

But Pim wasn't paying attention because Willow and Finchy kept playing with his utensils. Elle giggled but stopped when her eyes fell on the empty seat beside her. She missed Mike. It had already been a whole cycle without him. She has progressed so much and yet the feeling of triumph wasn't quite the same. She wondered where he might be, and she couldn't help but worry about whether he was okay or not.

Elle had no appetite and ended up just grabbing a few bites. After she had said goodnight to Sir Jon and Pim, she climbed the top dome where she'll be meeting her third cycle teacher.

Once inside, Elle sat on the floor in the middle of the room and waited patiently. Time passed and her neck was starting to feel strained, but no one arrived. Something felt wrong and that's when her eyes widened. What if something had happened to him?

Elle walked briskly toward the back door that led to another dome and politely knocked. "Master?" she called out. "Is everything alright?"

She waited a moment for an answer, but there was no reply. She tried to knock again with urgency. Nothing. Elle took a deep breath and turned the doorknob. It was unlocked.

"Master, I'm coming in, okay?" she said before letting herself in.

It was pitch black inside, so she reached for the sidewall to check if there was a light switch, but her hand didn't feel anything.

It was as if the doorframe was standing in the middle of nowhere.

"Master, are you in here?" she called out.

Still, no answer. Only the breeze came to whistle in her ear. *Where is this gust coming from?* The wind began to lash out harder, making her lean forward to keep her feet on the ground. The sound of her heartbeat drummed in her ears and fear flowed in her veins making the very ends of her skin prickle. Darkness embraced her, but Elle pushed on and kept walking farther until she came face to face with a gigantic white deer-shaped tree the size of a two-story house. Four of its roots stood like legs. In the midsection was a trunk where the roots merged to form a body, and on top of that was the shape of a neck and a head with ears and a muzzle that protruded. On top of its head were branches that gracefully arched, forming what looked like a set of antlers with an array of yellowish leaves.

Elle gaped in awe at the utter size and beauty of the creature. It was definitely something she has never seen before.

The strong winds mellowed down when the white tree suddenly moved. There was the sound of snapping timber and bark, and the leaves on its antlers rustled and fell down with the breeze as the Deer Tree's head looked down on her.

On top of one antler, Elle noticed a bird that had a striking shade of blue. It had the same shade as the dress she usually wore.

The bird flew in front of her and perched on her forearm just like Finchy often did.

Elle admired its feathers as it quietly sang. It's chirping drew her in, making her stare into its beady blue eyes. But there was something wrong. She was starting to feel lightheaded. Something about this tiny creature was making her head throb and her insides hurt.

"Stop! Stop it please!" Elle screamed.

She covered her ears. It was intolerable, and she knew she had to get away from it.

Elle bolted for the door. *Almost there!* She could see the tunnel-like light cast its rays inside the dark place. Elle's vision started to blur as she staggered towards it. She had barely made it out. She collapsed the moment her foot had stepped through the door.

When Elle came to, she sat up and rubbed her forehead. She was able to escape, but only by the crosshairs. Elle paused for a second to think. *What was that?* But then again, maybe she was asking the wrong question. *"Who" was that?*

Carefully, Elle lifted herself up and went back through the doorway. It was still dark inside. She noticed that the gusts of wind and the singing of the blue bird were gone. She took it as a good sign and walked back toward the giant Deer Tree.

Elle bowed her head. "Hello, Master," she said.

"Ah, you know who I am?" asked the Deer Tree in a voice so old it could have been around for more than a thousand years.

Elle nodded. "Luna once told me that sometimes Knowledge hides in the shadows."

"I have my reasons," said its thundering voice.

"I see. Well, will our trainings be held here then?" she asked.

"The Sky Dweller is not ready," the tree replied.

"I can try harder. I promise, I know I can do better next time."

"I have done everything I could to help you transcend, but your form keeps resisting. If we proceed, then you will most certainly die. That said, I bid you farewell."

The deer turned, its legs positioned to leave.

"That's it?" Elle blurted out. "It can't be. I've come all this way and… Just. Please, I need to finish my training. I will do anything. I'm ready for it, even if it kills me."

Knowledge looked back down at her. "Oh I know you would.

But what good is that?"

The deer leaned down and flipped his head. Its antler caught Elle in the stomach and flung her painfully out of the door. Hurriedly, Elle picked herself up but the door had already slammed shut. She tried to open it again, but once it did, what lay in front of her was just a plain backroom storage area. It was gone, the dark never-ending space where Knowledge could be found.

§

Elle slumped on the floor and clutched her stomach. She tried to reason with her emotions. *I can't just give up*. She felt disoriented and was maybe even seeing things. She rubbed her eyes and noticed that her shadow started to stretch out all the way to the wall.

What in the world… What's happening?

Elle sprang up and peered outside the glass dome. She noticed that the sun was moving. It was closing in so fast that she could see the moon's cheek overlapping the sun. It was an eclipse. Just as Luna had told her. It was the only time that she got to see her brother. And in all those eclipses, Luna had fought against Sunny.

From the water orb, Luna appeared, seemingly unaware of any danger. But once inside, she immediately caught a glimpse of the sky. By then Elle was already running to get Jon Bulbutton.

Luna's eyes locked with Elle. There were no words, but they understood each other and knew exactly what they had to do.

Elle entered their dome and found Jon stowing away his carving tools.

"Sir Jon!" she called out. "Come with me, quickly! The wolf is on his way."

The capybara looked horrified. "What? But how?"

"Luna has been followed," she said. "I'm going to hide you, and then we're going to escape though the water orb."

Elle cradled the frightened capybara in a blanket. It only took a couple of knots for her to create a makeshift backpack.

"Willow, Kick, Finchy, we need to leave fast!" she ordered while carrying Jon on her back.

Elle grabbed her belongings. Outside, the sky was growing darker by the minute.

She saw one of her teachers ringing a huge bell vigorously to alert every one of the arrival of the wolf. The deer folk who came out of their domes were armed and ready, their arrows aimed at the water orb.

Elle ran towards it. There was no other choice. Their only means of escape was also the only entrance from which Sunny could appear.

She was just a few meters away when a man leaped out from the portal. Arrows rained on him but they where easily dodged.

The man's nose wrinkled up as he sniffed the air, his head tilting toward Elle.

"Hello brother," Luna said. "Have you come for me or for something else?"

Sunny grunted. "Run away while you still can, dear," he said. "You have no idea of the power I have now. None of you can possibly stop me."

He held up his lyre, an instrument that had strings attached to a crossbar, and with his right hand, he drew out three huge arrows from his quiver. He loaded the arrows onto the strings of the lyre like a crossbow. Elle wasn't quite sure how he managed to use a musical instrument as a weapon, but the arrows shot straight toward her.

Elle dipped low and didn't stand until she heard the arrows swoop past her. It was a good thing Mike had taught her that move.

Sunny started reloading again, but the next set of arrows he shot were intercepted by Luna's blade. It was a perfect swing, and the arrows broke in half in midair.

"Is that all you've got?" Luna taunted.

Elle sensed that Luna was trying to distract him, giving her a window for escape. It was now or never. Elle darted for the orb. The Deer Folk continued to attack and corner him, but he was able to steer clear of each strike without even flinching. Elle could see that he had a sly grin on his face like everything was child's play. His features were similar to Luna's but there was that gleaming overconfidence in him.

"Where do you think you're going?" he said. "Come over here!"

Sunny started strumming his lyre with his long fingers. The sound was brisk and melodious, dreamlike and wicked. Slowly, he latched the lyre to his back and took out his sword from its scabbard. Elle was making her escape but the moment she heard the music, her feet started to march toward Sunny, like a child that followed a Pied Piper. It was happening all over again, that thing she experienced back in the Headmaster's office.

Under the shade of the full eclipse, Luna continued to fight head on.

"You can't possibly—" she mouthed in confusion. "That's dark magic! Stop! Or you'll be banished!"

"And who's going to banish me?" he said as he laughed. "You? I could have her stab herself too you know," he continued. "If only I didn't need her alive. Darn my luck!"

Luna stood her ground, blocking Elle's path. "Finchy!" she called out. "Get them out of here NOW!" Luna raised her left hand and opened the orb's portal.

"Not if I can't help it," Sunny said as he shape-shifted into a gigantic grey wolf. Its eyes were yellowish like the sun.

Finchy quickly sprang out of Elle's satchel and grew into a large finch. He swooped Elle onto his back and took her out through the water orb.

Upon arriving on the other side, above the snow-laden forest, Elle found herself able to move at will again.

"Are you alright?" Finchy asked. Elle snapped herself out from a daze and shook her head. "Finchy, thank you."

"Thank me later," he said, "Right now, the wolf is still on our tracks."

"I have a plan. Finchy, can you fly over the sea along the east? We need to find my mother before Sunny catches up to us. I think that she could help us create an illusion that could hide Jon Bulbutton. I doubt if she'll be staying at the house, knowing that I'll be gone for three cycles."

"Okay," he said.

Finchy found a stream and followed its path that would lead them to the sea.

"I can see it," Elle blurted out, "the open water over on the horizon!"

But Finchy was distracted by something else. "Umm, Elle, I think we're being followed."

Elle peered down and found the trees swaying in the path parallel to theirs.

"Oh dear," Jon Bulbutton said from inside the blanket on Elle's back. "This is not good!"

All of a sudden, Finchy began to tilt sideways that Elle had to clutch tightly onto his feathers. There was that sound again. It was the music from the lyre.

Elle was starting to slide off the finch's back. "Finchy! Snap out of it! It's Sunny, he's trying to control you. You have to fight it!"

The finch didn't respond. Instead, he flipped her completely upside down. Elle felt her grip slide off from Finchy's silky feathers, and all she could hear was Jon saying the words, "Oh dear, oh dear, oh dear." Before she knew it, she was falling from the sky.

Her gut felt like it had gone straight up her throat, and she was about to crash down in the trees when a large group of griffins rose from the forest.

One of them lunged up and caught her on its back with a loud thump. The griffin made a shrill eagle cry as she sat atop the back of its muscular lion body. Elle immediately checked on the blanket behind her back.

"Are you okay, Sir Jon?"

"Oh my!" he replied. "Yes, yes, yes. I think I'm fine. Oh! Amos! That was a good catch!"

Elle looked closely at the griffin and immediately recognized the hieroglyph markings on its body and squealed, "Amos!"

"Yeah, it's me. Nice to have you guys *drop* in," Amos said jokingly.

"You need to help us. Sunny is on our tail," Jon Bulbutton said.

"Sunny? Well, I don't think any wolf in its right mind is going to attack a pack of griffins, Sir Jon. We're leagues more powerful than wolves."

Elle looked back at the horizon and saw the pack of graceful griffins soaring alongside them.

Finchy was there too, gliding nearby.

"I'm sorry, Elle," he said. "I don't know what just happened!"

"It's okay, Finchy," she replied. "I know it wasn't your fault."

Amos nodded. "It's all good now. Lock it in, bro," he said, extending his closed talons to give Finchy a fist bump.

"Your timing was perfect, Amos!" Elle said as she hugged the griffin.

"Yeah, I felt my Sky Dweller senses tingling and came as fast as I could," he said as if he were a superhero, which made Elle laugh.

"My pack and I were actually on our way to Higher Gan for the *Feast of the Guardians*. It's in a few days, and we were called in to help with a few things. We could all head there now if you want."

"Oh but—" Elle mumbled in an undertone. "I need to find my mother first. You see, we're helping Jon Bulbutton, and I think my mom could help us hide him for a while."

"I see. Yeah, Mike told me everything about Jon and Sunny and that girl who turned herself into a tree. I think I know just the place where your mom could be," Amos said.

As they flew, Amos ordered the other griffins to capture the sun wolf while they tried to find Emilia.

Amos continued to soar until they reached a sulfur-rich pond. There were layers of crystal-like formations and the pools of water steamed misty white, making her vision blurry. Elle kept wiping her eyes as she sprinted toward the water. "Excuse me," she called out urgently to one of the mermen. "I'm looking for my mother. Her name's Emilia. Would you know where I could find her?"

From a distance, Elle heard her mother's voice.

"Elle? Is that you?" Emilia swam up to her and smiled so excitedly that even her tail fins seemed to wag. "Oh, look at my girl! You're shaping up really well."

"Uhm, thank you. Mom, have you heard about the wolf chasing Sir Jon Bulbutton?"

"Of course, I have," her mom replied. "It's quite sad. Hmm. Why? Are you hiding him, dear?"

"Yes," answered Elle. "Actually, I was wondering if you could help hide him for us until things get sorted out. I'm sure he could build a wonderful statue for the merpeople while he's with you. Just like he did for Luna."

“Alright dear. Is there anything else? Oh! Wait a minute. What is that? You’re carrying a sword?”

“Yes. Luna gave me Eve’s Land Dweller Whilom. Come to think of it, Mom, would you know where I could find the others?” she asked.

“Oh,” her mom sighed drearily. “Eve’s Sea Dweller Whilom. I have a hunch, but I honestly don’t know. Also, getting it won’t be easy, sweetheart. I don’t recommend it.”

Elle remembered how some Sea Dwellers developed psychic abilities. Who knows, her mom could be right and right now, her hunch was her best bet.

“It’s something I have to do, Mom. The Tree of Life told me that I must collect all four.”

“Okay,” Emilia said. “If there is no other choice then I might as well help you. I’ll come over to the house tomorrow. I’ll have to prepare some things you’ll need. And by the way, please wear something proper and fix that hair of yours. Tomorrow, I will need you to try and blend in with us merpeople. I think I’ll be able to disguise you so you’d look like one of us.”

“Okay. Thanks, Mom!” Elle said. She hugged her, then freed the capybara from the blanket. Jon wiggled his way out and stretched his cramped muscles before shaking hands with Emilia.

“Pleased to meet you, Madame.”

“Hi, Sir Jon. It is my honor. Now come, we must hurry.”

“Thank you, Emilia. I will not take your kindness for granted,” replied the capybara as he followed her.

“We must be going now, too,” Elle said, “I’ll see you tomorrow, Mom.”

Elle hopped back onto Amos’ back.

“It was nice to meet you, Elle’s mom,” Amos said, bowing courteously before flying up to regroup with his pack.

“Could you fly me back home?” Elle asked Amos. “Just to be sure Finchy doesn’t get compromised again.”

“Of course,” Amos exclaimed. “Shall I also turn on the taxi meter, mademoiselle?”

“Yeah, I guess you can, if you had one,” Elle chortled.

One of the griffins flew up to Amos. “We lost the sun wolf.”

“How does he always get to slip away?” asked Amos. “Look, the pack will have to stand guard tonight.”

CHAPTER SIXTEEN

- Mike -

There was a fresco just behind Big Ben's desk. A wall-to-wall, hand-painted map of Eden. It had been there for as long as Mike could remember. On the lower right were markings of two golden handprints.

Mike took out a can of gold paint, dipped his palm in and pressed his hand beside his mother's, his pinky slightly overlapping with hers. He knew, without a doubt, that his parents had the time of their lives as they drew up all sorts of maps. They had explored worlds together, laughed together, and dreamed together.

After wiping off his gold-painted hands, Mike levitated towards the north part of the map where he added the words *Land of the Deer Folk*.

He then glanced at it from afar. There was the land of flying squirrels and the deer folk on the north side, Upper and Higher Gan at the heart, then Bulbutton Square down south. Then to the east was the Tree of Life, and farther east still lay Atlantis. As for the west, there was nothing. It was utterly barren. A dessert where no living creature had wanted to dwell in. Mike felt like he had to explore it one of these days.

He got back down on his feet and was about to stow away his father's paint when he heard a familiar swishing sound by the balcony. Only a Sky Dweller with four wings could make a sound like that.

"Any news, Erin?" Mike asked before even glancing in her direction.

Erin walked in wearing a pristine white sleeveless jumpsuit with scabbards that held her swords and daggers in place. "Luna is being healed at this very moment. I had to ask the Tree of Life for help. She was attacked by Sunny."

Mike felt his chest tighten. "Was she outside of the Deer Camp when it happened? Is Elle okay?"

Erin rolled her eyes, "Oh. Your girlfr—"

Before Erin could finish, Mike had already leaped off the balcony.

He had felt her presence. She had to be near.

Mike flew straight toward the yellow house and found griffins lying around the garden.

The front door had swung open. It was Amos. Shirtless like always to show off his ink, his dreadlocks were bouncing as he walked down the front steps.

"Yo' Bro! Check out what I found!" he said.

Behind him, Elle appeared. Mike didn't know what came over him, but he couldn't stop himself. He went straight for Elle and held her.

"Mike, I'm glad to see that you're okay," he heard her say.

"Silly girl," he said in reply. "I'm the one who should be worried about you."

"Oh hey, Erin!" Elle blurted out as she broke away from him.

Erin had just landed not long after Mike did.

"Why don't you guys come inside," Elle said. "Umm… I need to ask for your help."

Mike sat down beside Elle on the sofa while Amos lounged on the woven carpet. Erin closed the door behind her and leaned beside the windowsill as if she had already calculated her immediate escape for worst-case scenarios.

"So," Elle said as she poured some tea for Mike and Erin, "here's what I think about the whole Sunny situation. If he really is working for the Serpent, then he's not just after Jon Bulbutton. He'll be after me, too. And for some reason, he needs me alive. I'm guessing it's because he has no clue as to where to find the Whiloms."

"Yeah," Amos said, shaking his head. "We're not going to let him have them."

Elle nodded.

"Exactly. We need to find the other three Whiloms immediately before Sunny beats us to it," she said, handing them their tea. "And his mind control doesn't work on you guys. I thought I'd be able to do the same after getting some training, but I was wrong. I'm still as vulnerable to dark magic as I was before I came here."

"Don't worry Elle," Mike said sensing the anxiety in her voice. "We'll help you."

Erin crossed her arms together and paced back and forth. "It's going to be hard," she said, "We've been trying to hunt him down, and he keeps finding a way out."

Amos lay down on the carpet. "Oh, he's definitely going to follow us around."

§

Mike couldn't sleep—probably none of them could. Elle and Erin were in the bedroom while he and Amos took the living room carpet and the couch.

Every time Mike closed his eyes, he'd relive those last few seconds he'd had with his dad, alternating with those few minutes of fending off the dragon. He had to be fearless. He had been, so far, but whenever it was about Elle, everything inside him got jumbled up.

Who was he kidding? Of course, he always wanted to protect her no matter what. But that line of thinking might be dangerous. It could change his priorities completely. His stomach churned at the thought of having her face danger alone. No. He took deep breaths to calm himself. He had trained her, and she was going to have to deal with danger alone at some point. He just had to believe in her.

§

Emilia arrived first thing in the morning. After having breakfast, she promptly prepped them on what to expect when they finally ventured into Atlantis.

Amos had also relieved his fellow griffins from their guard duties to fly out to Higher Gan and help out in preparation for the festivities while the rest of them stayed for the mission to retrieve Eve's Sea Dweller Whilom.

"This better be done before the Feast of the Guardians," Amos said, "or we'll all be in big trouble."

Elle's mom rolled her eyes, in a manner that said that she couldn't care less. Emilia wore her usual strips of deep green colored cloth wrapped around her body. The fabric was very much like silk and had white seashells attached to it. She also brought similar garments for Elle and Erin to wear. Mike tried his best not to look at Elle without his blood pumping double-time. She had a sheer blue material wrapped around her and almost nothing underneath. It was layered in the right places to cover just enough. Emilia was ecstatic that she was able to dress up and fix her daughter's hair with intricate braids and ornaments.

Elle was obviously not comfortable with the whole get-up. "Umm… Mom, I think that's enough. We better get going soon," she said.

"Fine. Fine. Anyway, here we are," Emilia said as she motioned everyone to come closer. She took out a bagful of conch shells and handed one to each of them. It was slightly hefty with a siphonal canal and a spire at the top. The first thing Mike did was to check if there was a mollusk inside.

None. Good.

"These shells are a common device among Non-Sea Dwellers," continued Emilia. "It is used to breathe underwater. You only need to inhale once and you will be able to go on airless for about ten to fifteen minutes."

Emilia then showed them how to use it. "You breathe through this hole by pressing your lips like so, and you will be using this rope to strap the shell onto your waist so that it doesn't float away when it's time for you to catch your breath. All clear?"

They all nodded.

"Alright. Then let's go," she said.

They strolled toward the bay where Mike did a quick rundown

of *the plan*.

"Okay, everyone," he said. "I know that right now we're like fish out of water."

"Yeah, that's because we're going to be birds under water in just a few seconds," Amos said, bemused.

"I know! Well, there's a first time for everything," Mike replied. "I can only hope that we get things right the first try."

He gestured to his left. "Just to make sure we're all on the same page. Mrs. Emilia here will be the one tasked to distract potential Sea Dwellers who might pass by and see us."

He nodded his head in Emilia's direction to make sure she understood. "Next. The one in charge of obtaining the Whilom is going to be Elle. I honestly want to do this part, but since Elle here insisted on doing it, I will concede. It is your mission, and we are here to support you," Mike said as he gave a half-worried-smile before proceeding to Amos and Erin. "As for the three of us. We're going to secure the perimeter. Ward off any danger, and well, you know the drill. Let's all keep our eyes peeled for any suspicious movement. We're not sure if the sun wolf is capable of doing mind control from under the sea, so it's best to be very cautious."

They all agreed before heading toward the water.

"Okay," Emilia said. "Males, time to take off your shirts. Mermen don't wear them, FYI."

Mike figured that she meant him because the only shirt Amos ever really wore were his tattoos. He took off his shirt and dipped into the water just a few feet behind Elle and her mother. He breathed in deep and submerged himself after them.

The water was clear and a little warm from the sun. As he started to swim, he saw Emilia's fins glitter. The mermaid moved swiftly underwater, like she didn't feel the heavy drag and compression of the sea. Mike had to pop his ears as they swam deeper and inhaled from the conch shell once in a while.

His muscles started to ache as he continued to swim. They all found it hard to keep up with Emilia, and it didn't take long until she noticed it, too. Emilia turned to them and winked conspiratorially.

She swung her right arm in weird angles, and in seconds, an undercurrent pulled them further down. Mike kept an eye on everyone, making sure no one got hurt as they were dragged by the water.

Mike reached down for his conch shell that was floating along his knee. Good thing it was roped to his waist or else it would have drifted away. He quickly pressed it against his lips and inhaled.

That's when Emilia began speaking to them. Mike thought that it was just in his head, but then again, he knew that some merpeople were psychic in a way.

"Everyone," Emilia said. "Atlantis is just below. No matter what happens, just continue swimming!"

Mike peered down, but there was nothing unusual at all. There was only the same crystal-clear water and a seabed a few meters below. It had corals and seaweeds and boulders on the sand. They followed behind Emilia as the seabed drew nearer. He was somewhat prepared to hit his head on the corals at any moment. He took a deep breath from the conch shell and closed his eyes to brace for impact. But nothing happened.

Mike opened his eyes, bewildered. The corals, the seaweeds, and the sand just grew bigger and bigger as they sank deeper. It was the same seabed, but it had the illusion that it was shallow when it wasn't at all. He couldn't believe his eyes. On the corals were circular windows where he could see merpeople in their living quarters. Further down, he noticed that each grain of sand had actually been huge rocks.

Surrounding them was a colorful city, filled with grandeur

and ornamentation. Mike was immediately taken in by the view.

Again, Emilia waved her hand in precise angles, creating another current that whirled them down between two oddly shaped coral shelters.

"There it is," she exclaimed, pointing to a statue.

On an oval area that resembled a park were a bunch of sea anemones, moss, and spiny corals, which were laid out beautifully and symmetrically like a garden. At the center was a huge rock carved in the shape of a proud merman. There was a crown on his head, hair flowing, muscles bulging, and a face so strong it could command you with a mere stare. Below its massive fins there were smaller carvings of sea creatures and mermaids and shipwrecks, but the most magnificent of all was the trident in the merman's hand. It was shinier than gold—so polished that it looked like it had been made yesterday.

The park along the monument appeared to be desolate, and they all swam toward their designated positions. Emilia was on the lookout by the front pathway. Mike, Erin, and Amos were on guard by the sand dollar benches, their eyes peeled at the coral houses and the open water.

Mike checked on Elle from the corner of his eyes. He saw her swim up to the statue with both hands outstretched. Something felt wrong, and he knew it the moment Elle touched the trident. The ground gave a loud rumble, and they could feel the disturbance in the sway of the water. Time was ticking. Something big was definitely coming their way. Mike gripped his sword and glanced at Elle as she tried to pull the Whilom from the statue's hand. She anchored her leg onto the statue's arm for leverage until it finally gave way. *She did it! She's got the Trident!*

Mike's eyes grew as the statue began to crack. They were under water, and he couldn't scream and tell her to watch out. The

Merman's statue crumbled from the bottom up and crashed on the seabed.

Under the collapsed figure, the head of a giant eel came out.

Mike heard her muffled squeal as Elle swam in panic. He was swimming toward her when the giant eel snapped at her leg. Its open mouth was like a cave that could devour a man whole.

The next thing he knew, there came a cloud of red haze. It took a second for him to realize that it was blood gushing out from Elle's thigh. The eel had nipped her!

Mike couldn't see a thing, but he continued to swim toward her. When he finally spotted Elle, he saw that the rope wrapped around her waist was tugging her. *No way! Her conch shell, it's stuck in between the eel's teeth!* Elle tried to wriggle it off but the eel held its mouth shut. It started to grin as it tasted the iron from the bloodstained water. Mike pulled out his blade, ready to cut the rope.

The red haze was starting to clear out thanks to Emilia. In an instant, before Mike was able to grab the rope, he saw Emilia, horror-stuck, her mermaid hand stretched out to strike the eel. The creature saw her too, and instinctively retreated into the hole on the ground where the statue once stood, dragging Elle into the depths along with it. Everything seemed to run in slow motion as Mike tried to grab her. Her eyes connected with him and before he knew it, she was thrashing for air. It was too late. His hand could only clutch onto the dress flowing behind her. It tore in his hand, and then the next thing he knew, she disappeared into the dark gaping hole.

She's going to run out of air!

Mike tried to swim into the hole, but the water gushing out of it was too strong. Fizz kept lashing out, making it difficult to get in.

A few seconds later, it stopped. Mike tried again. In the deep darkness, he could see a dot of light. It was coming closer. It was speeding up, and he managed to move out of the way just in time as the giant eel writhed out of the hole yet again. This time, with Elle clutching tightly onto its back and the trident in her hand.

The Whilom glowed, and the eel, as if taking in Elle's command, slowly lifted her up toward the water's surface.

Around them, merpeople were starting to form a crowd, frightened but curious as they followed them above water.

Mike swam alongside Emilia, Amos, and Erin, who were all just as shaken. When they reached the surface, Mike felt relieved for being able to breathe again through his nostrils.

What came next took them all by surprise.

Mike couldn't believe his eyes when the terrifying eel changed form. As it started taking shape, the crowd began to cheer. Right before them, the beast had turned into a merman, and the merpeople suddenly boomed, "Long live Alon!"

Alon stretched out his arms and fins and laughed as loud as anyone could possibly laugh. He was huge and muscular, just like his image on the statue. His crown had the same golden gleam as the trident. Then Alon looked at Elle and reached out his hand to her.

"Thank you, dear girl. Now, would you be so kind as to hand over my trident?" he said.

"Oh. There must be a mistake," Elle mumbled back. "This… this trident is Eve's Whilom. I'm sorry but I simply cannot hand it over to you, sir."

"What?" he blurted out. "Who are you? And why do you need it?"

"I am Elle," she said. "Granddaughter of Adam and Eve. The Tree of Life was the one who gave me the task of collecting Eve's four Whiloms. So, if you will, I'd like to keep holding onto it."

"I see. Still, the trident is mine. This on the other hand, was hers," Alon plucked a pearl from his crown. "It was the hardest thing I've ever had to take. Do you know what this tiny little pearl is?"

"Is that her Whilom?" she asked.

Alon nodded. "This pearl. It is a treasure that has taken far too many lives."

Mike blinked in disbelief and decided to swim beside Elle to make sure nothing went wrong. She glanced back at him, clearly confused.

"You see, Atlantis is a great city," continued Alon, "and I simply cannot allow Eve to destroy my life's work. I knew she would come for us. So, I prepared for her arrival."

His eyes prodded them, seeking some kind of assurance that he had done the right thing. "I created a sequence of illusions to steal the pearl from her. I will not say how, for it is a secret I cannot tell. She had to be in her human form for me to take it, and when she took the bait, I managed to replace her pearl with a decoy while embedding hers into my crown before her dark magic turned me into a mindless man-eating monster. Then she left me… to destroy the Atlantis that I had built from the ground up. I could see it all happening right in front of me, but I couldn't stop myself. She turned me into a monster."

Elle looked grave. She shook her head. She didn't want to believe in the atrocities the dragon had done to Eden. It was her grandmother or that Serpent that had mind-controlled Alon.

"The elder Midians were the ones who trapped me under that hole," Alon said, "to save my own city without having to kill me. I could only be freed, once the curse has been lifted. And for that, I am greatly indebted to you, Elle."

Alon bowed to her. "Thank you for freeing me. But I shall be needing my trident to lead my people."

Elle hesitated a little. "Before I hand it over, can I first take a closer look at the pearl?"

Alon lowered his hand closer to Elle. She inspected it, and so did Mike.

"It has the same dragon's head marking etched on its surface," she said before nodding resolutely. "Okay. A trade then. Your trident in exchange for that pearl."

"You do not understand child," Alon said. "I cannot simply entrust the pearl to you. In fact, I can take that trident from your hand with a flick of a finger," he laughed mockingly. "So, there will be no exchange. You must understand. Eve used it to wreak havoc in our world. And to think she used to be a wonderful person. It cannot possibly be safe in just anybody's hand. Yes, as her descendant, you may have been the only one who could have freed me. Still, that doesn't change the conditions that befall us. I can only give you one favor, and that is it."

"One favor. Then I ask that you give me a chance to prove myself," implored Elle. "Give me a test that if I pass, I get the pearl that belongs to my family."

Alon paused to consider. "Hmmm. You've got guts, kid," he said. "As an Atlantean leader—I cannot believe I'm saying this—but I accept your proposal. You may be the grandchild of the dragon, but there is also Adam's blood flowing inside of you. So yes, maybe we'll see if you are indeed as strong and as good as he."

Alon reached out his hand, and instantly, the trident gravitated toward him. "You and your friends may stay at the airlock. It's where we keep our guests. For now, I will let you rest and then I'll give you your task tomorrow." He gestured to Emilia. "Kindly lead the Sky Dwellers to the airlock."

They all followed Emilia as she swam toward a coral palace.

One at a time, they entered a tube that stuck out from one side of the stronghold.

Mike slid down the tube where he felt hot air blowing in from the sides. He was dry the moment he landed inside. "It's safe, you can all come down," he shouted into the tube.

The size of the airlock hub was massive. The floor glittered with crushed corals, the walls were studded with vertical gardens for oxygen, and the ceiling and pillars were just as ornate as the pearls of a mermaid. At the middle of the hall stood something that resembled a statue, or more like an unfinished statue of the Triad. Mike tilted his head up as he gazed at the faces of the three leaders of Eden: Alon, Adam, and his father, Ben Gabriel. The great Midians who embodied the best of their kind, and whose voices became the voice for their people.

Clank! Clank! Mike veered his attention toward the noise. Entering the hall was Jon Bulbutton looking busy as ever. "Sir Jon?" asked Mike.

Elle, Amos, Erin, and Emilia came in through the tube right behind him.

The capybara's whiskers shivered in his surprise, dropping a chisel. "Well blimey! Mike and Elle! What are you two doing here in Atlantis? You youngsters must be checking up on how I am." Jon picked up his chisel. "As you can see, dearies, I try to keep myself preoccupied." Jon stowed the multitude of tools he had been carrying onto a table. "You fellows came just in time for supper. I'm sure you're all quite hungry."

As he led them to the banquet, he turned to Elle. "I don't think I've had the chance to thank you properly, Elle," he said, holding Elle's hand in his. "I'm very grateful for all your help." He peered at their companions. "Amos and Erin, hmmm. Are you two here to visit me, too?"

"We're here to retrieve one of Eve's Whiloms, Sir Jon," replied Erin.

"Ah, yes," Jon said. "Of course. Well, good luck with that."

The long dinner table was filled with the most unusual food they had ever seen—some were slimy, others glowed in the dark, and others burst goo—but they were famished from all the swimming that it didn't seem to matter how the dishes looked or tasted like.

After wolfing down the food, Emilia led them to their quarters where they each had their own room.

CHAPTER SEVENTEEN

- Elle -

Elle sat on top of the bed while her mother placed a green jelly-like substance over her leg wound, the one that had been scraped by the eel's sharp teeth.

"I told you. This was a bad idea to begin with," her mom grunted. "I don't know what Alon has in store for you tomorrow, but I dread what might happen if you don't succeed."

Elle leaned in and placed a hand on her mother's shoulder. "Then I won't fail."

Emilia nodded and kissed her daughter's forehead before standing up to leave. "You better not fail. Now get some rest," she said, closing the door behind her.

Elle slumped her sore body onto the water bed. The air was getting so stuffy in the airlock that she started feeling lightheaded. Out from the concave window, Elle saw merpeople and sea creatures of different shapes and sizes treading happily along the water. It was a wonderful scenery, and it was vastly different from the world above. Everything looked so calm and dreamlike that it lulled her to sleep.

§

The next day, Elle woke up with a slight headache. She peered out of the window, or in this case, the airlock's thick pressurized concave glass window. Unfortunately, what she saw was far from the beautiful calm scenery that she had seen before falling asleep. Elle jumped to her feet in a wave of shock. Out in the open, she saw merpeople floating in a daze. Every single one of them was motionless and had a distant stare. *What's going on?* Elle ran out of the room and checked the other quarters only to find them empty. She started to feel panic well up inside of her.

Elle picked up her conch shell and left the airlock through an exit tube. *Mom! Jon! Mike! Erin! Amos! Where is everybody? All those Sea Dwellers… this could only be Sunny's doing. He must have found a way to get here.*

Instantly, she was rocketed out to the deep sea. Bodies. Piles and piles of merpeople floating without direction. Their eyes were blank like their minds had been frozen. Elle bumped into a couple of them as she headed for the main castle.

There it is. Alon must be in there fighting Sunny!

But as she got near the castle, a dark shadow loomed over her head. Elle felt goosebumps prickle her skin as she craned her neck up. There was a dragon on the castle's pinnacle.

Elle swam up as fast as she could. She had to find a way to draw the dragon out of Atlantis. The dragon tilted its head toward her direction and spoke. A soft female voice reverberated in her head, "My precious, darling Uriel."

She was so dumbfounded that she stopped swimming altogether.

"Shall I take you up in the sky where you belong?" the dragon said.

Its body moved like a snake as it sped toward her. Before she could protest, she found herself against the dragon's nostrils, being pushed upward, away from Atlantis.

Once above the water Elle crawled on top of the dragon's back and the first words that came out of her mouth were, "Are you my grandmother? Are you Eve? I find all this hard to process right now."

"Yes dear, it's me. I managed to survive, and I came here to protect you. Contrary to what most people think, Alon is actually a lot more dangerous than you think," the dragon said.

Elle's eyebrows furrowed. "It's you who's dangerous. Please, Grandma, if there's an ounce of good left in you, then you'd undo that hex you did on those Sea Dwellers! At first, I thought it was Sunny behind all this, but now I'm a hundred percent sure it's because of you!"

The dragon then started to spread its wings, slowly lifting them up in the air. "There's no need to worry, Uriel. Everyone is now back to the way they were."

They breezed along, casting an ominous shadow along the sea. Elle was so focused on getting the dragon out of Atlantis that she didn't quite figure out what she'll do afterwards.

"Where are we going?" she asked nervously.

"There's something I want to show you, dear."

They settled down on a deserted island that had crystal slopes glistening along the sides. It created a rainbow-like projection onto its surroundings.

"I have a gift that I want to give you," the dragon said.

Elle walked alongside Eve as they entered the crystalline cave.

Along the entrance was a pile of bones stacked up on the side. The very idea of it gave her a fright that her heart started thumping wildly in her chest.

The pile of bones was curved into a hollow dome. At the middle stood a crystal-like fruit, its seed gleaming red from the inside. The dragon sat beside her.

"Elle, this will help you transcend. I'm giving you this chance so that you can be so much more. Wouldn't you like that? It will help you become a real Sky Dweller just exactly how you should be."

"No," Elle found herself saying. "I don't want a poisoned fruit that is wrapped with false promises. I don't want to be a dragon like you. The answer is no," she said with finality.

"Then you leave me no choice." The dragon inhaled deep, preparing to breathe fire.

Elle staggered toward the cave's exit and heard flames crackle behind her.

She turned and found something black and furry blocking her view. It had taken the hit, shielding her from the fire. When Elle got a hold of herself, she realized that it was a huge ape that had saved her. That face. Those eyes. They reminded her of her grandpa.

The ape crashed to the ground. "Run!" he pleaded, urging her escape as his body continued to catch fire, but Elle couldn't leave him.

The dragon was about to unleash another searing breath.

"No!" Elle screamed out loud, her hand stretched out in front of Eve. Her face was riddled with a different kind of rage and fury as she saw the life drain out of the ape's eyes.

"Grandpa," Elle breathed out.

"What now, dear?" Eve asked. "Do you surrender? Are you

now ready to eat the fruit?"

"No," she replied, the word seething between her clenched teeth.

Elle unsheathed the Tranquil Blade from its scabbard. She started to emit white energy and was completely bathed in light. Blue wings began to spread from her back, and she floated as wind gushed around her like a tornado. Swiftly, the dragon attacked and gnawed its sharp teeth at her, but it was futile.

Up close, Elle was able to see into the dragon's inverted eyes, and she realized what she had to do.

She gave all of herself into the Tranquil Blade and raised it to the sky. Light consumed everything around her, and she felt her soul drift away. She was going to die just as Gabriel had. She was a Sky Dweller, fulfilling every Sky Dweller's fate.

§

Elle woke up enclosed inside a glass capsule.

No.

It was more like she was sealed off in a round coffin.

"What the—hey! I'm not dead!" Elle shouted as she pounded onto the glass.

"Look! She's awake!" cried a little girl.

There was a crowd of merpeople, hundreds of them, sitting and floating in rows of large half-opened shells that resembled the painting of the Birth of Venus.

"What's going on? Alon!" Elle called out when she saw him swim toward the capsule.

"Relax and breathe slowly or you'll faint," Alon said. "This capsule can only provide a limited amount of oxygen."

"I'm not sure I can do that right now," Elle replied. "Alon, why am I here?"

Alon gave her a hopeful smile. "We have deliberated and concluded that you, Elle, have proven yourself worthy. You have passed the test."

"What? You mean, all that happened was part of some test? I thought I died. That couldn't have been an illusion. It felt so real."

Elle breathed harder, shocked by how everything had turned out. Her heart sank when she realized that her transcendence had been fake, but she was relieved that she had passed.

Elle looked around and was able to find Mike, Erin, and Amos, watching from the balcony. They were breathing from conch shells. She wanted to wave at them, but she felt exhausted and particularly dizzy from the lack of oxygen.

"I need to keep my eyes open. I have to—"

CHAPTER EIGHTEEN

- Mike -

Mike swam as fast as he could when Elle fainted. By the time he reached her, Alon had already used his trident to take Elle out of the capsule. She floated in the water, her dress, half-torn, drifting wistfully around her.

In Alon's left hand, the pearl glowed bright in the form of a necklace. It drifted toward Elle and locked itself around her neck.

"She has done well," Alon said, his eyes steady on her. "The world needs more people like her. Now go and take her. I will not waste any more of her time."

Mike cradled Elle in his arms. He wanted to thank Alon, but he couldn't speak under water.

"Farewell, Sky Dwellers. Le-Ovedah," Alon said as he lifted his trident and swooshed them toward the surface. Erin and Amos came afloat shortly after him.

The moment they caught air, Mike checked for Elle's pulse. It was beating steadily. Her breathing was normal too.

"She's okay," Mike said.

"Alright. Now, we better start heading over to Higher Gan," Erin said.

"Last one there is a rotten egg!" shouted Amos.

§

Elle was still unconscious when they arrived in Higher Gan. The only thing Mike was concerned about was getting her to safety, but upon reaching the gates, the first thing he saw was the elder, Umi, awaiting their arrival. She was a very small old lady with a pointy nose and wings that flapped so fast they were practically invisible. Umi was a hummingbird Sky Dweller; she may be very small but she was fierce.

"Michael," she called out.

Mike bowed his head, "Lady Umi. I—"

The elder had raised her hand and said, "I need to speak with you."

She turned around and darted for the balcony that led to an assembly room. When she glanced back at him, she said, "Now," in a tone that was not to be trifled with.

Mike handed Elle over to his friends.

"Please make sure she's okay," he said firmly before heading after Lady Umi.

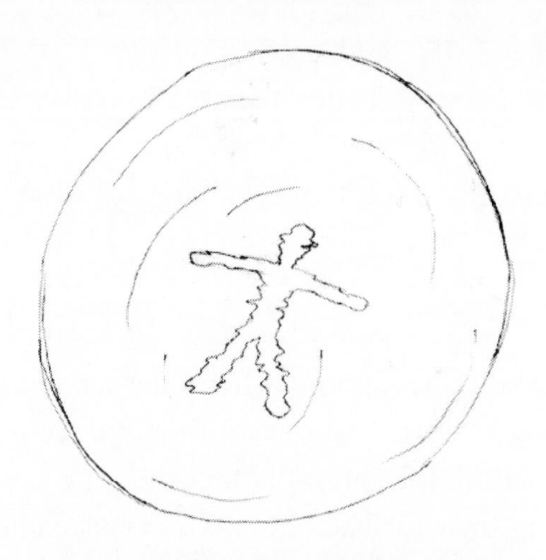

CHAPTER NINETEEN

- Elle -

When Elle came to, she found herself inside an enormous church-like room. The place was bright with intricate sculptures of Sky Dwellers that stood with hands held high to lift the ceiling up. *Am I back at Mike's castle? I don't remember it being THIS beautiful.*

She fumbled around for her belongings. On the bedside table was the Tranquil Blade. Upon sitting up, Elle felt something dangle around her neck. She looked down. It was the pearl with the dragon marking. She held it in her hand and wondered what it could possibly do since every Whilom had its own power that was meant to help Midians.

Outside the window was a cloudy sky. It was still a pleasant day—a stark contrast compared to the numbing cold water of Atlantis. It was hard to process everything that had happened—from the time when she had freed Alon from the curse, up until she had proven herself worthy of the pearl.

She clasped her hand to her face when she remembered Willow, Kick and Finchy. She had missed their liveliness. They were probably still at the house worried sick. Elle glanced at the door. Someone had been knocking.

"Hey, you're awake," Erin said as she entered. "How are you feeling?"

"I'm alright," Elle replied. She was a little surprised that Erin appeared to be friendlier than usual towards her. "Umm. Where are we?"

"Before anything, you better drink this," Erin said as she handed her a glass of water and laid a plate of biscuits on the table beside her.

"Right now, we're in Higher Gan," she said. "It's the Feast of the Guardians today so please come down to the Great Hall once you're ready. I also brought you something to wear for the celebration. It's over there." She pointed to the chair where a dress was splayed out.

"I'm surprised that you were able to pull it off, Elle. It was a brave thing you did back in Atlantis. I guess I was wrong about you. Anyway, the important thing is that you're okay now."

"Erin, thank you," Elle said. "I really hope we could be good friends."

"Yeah. I hope so too."

"By the way, will Mike be here too? In Higher Gan?"

"Yeah, about that. I need to talk to you about Mike," Erin said as she sat on the bed beside her. "You see, he's been on the edge lately. He worries about you all the time and then he needs to juggle his duties, too. Mike has done exceptionally well, but when it comes to you, he gets flustered. It's like he can't be as objective whenever you're the one involved and it makes him commit a few errors in judgment. I'm not sure if you're aware of it, but I really think he's taken by you. He's almost like a brother to me so his behavior worries me a little. I hope he gets to sort things out, whatever tangle he has in that silly head. But I don't know, maybe it's just me."

"Of course, I understand," replied Elle. "We all have to watch out for the people we care about. Thank you for telling me this Erin."

"Yeah. I really hope everything works out fine. Well, I better get going so you could get ready. The Great Hall is just downstairs, it's pretty easy to find."

Erin smiled warmly and turned to leave.

Elle took a good look at the dress. It was the right size. The material also had pieces of armor in it. Pretty cool. Elle slid it on and checked the mirror. At that moment, her heart had skipped a beat. She looked like a real Sky Dweller who was geared up for battle. Elle felt as if she had grown a few years older since the day she left Hillworth. Even though she hadn't successfully transcended yet, she knew that she had at the very least achieved becoming a warrior.

When Elle left the room, she padded down a carpeted staircase and found her way toward the Great Hall. The place was filled with Midians who watched the proceedings on stage. Elle sat on one of the empty tables nearest the entrance and curiously observed her surroundings.

Sky Dwellers were sitting amongst each other, facing the podium where a small old lady stood with wings flapping faster than her eyes could catch.

"Michael, son of Ben Gabriel, please come forth," the old lady said.

Mike was there and he came up on stage. His eyes firm and collected as he approached the elder lady.

"As we all know," the elder said. "it was Michael who freed Eve from her bonds. It came at a great cost, but he has persevered. And today, in honor of the fallen Sky Dwellers, we pass on the torch."

She faced Mike and took out her sword. "Please kneel."

Mike knelt and bowed his head.

"To you Michael, we entrust His army," the old lady said as she dubbed him like a knight. "Archangel Michael, may you lead us to victory. I pray you have safe travels in Gethsemane. Le-Ovedah."

The Sky Dwellers were all clapping and nodding their heads.

"My dear Midians! Let us celebrate! Victory awaits us!"

Archangel? So, he really was growing into his father's shoes. Archangel Gabriel had been His Messenger, and now, Michael had just been appointed to command a whole army. He is practically EVERYONE'S guardian! He must feel the weight of the world upon him now—just as I had felt when I first arrived in Eden with a promise of who I had to be.

Mike bowed facing the crowd and when he raised his head, his eyes fell on Elle. There was no denying it. He had to look brave for everyone's sake—even hers.

Two armored Sky Dwellers came up to him and patted him proudly on the back. Mike nodded to them.

"I'm ready," he declared. They paced toward a crater at the middle of the floor. It looked almost like a glassy planetarium that illuminated from within. *It must be the Gethsemane the elder was talking about.* The Sky Dwellers assisted him as Mike lay down and closed his eyes. Mike's body drifted to the middle, creating a slow ripple in space and time.

The elder spoke again to address the crowd. "Thank you all for your presence. Our dear Michael will be spending some time in Gethsemane, so let us pray that he makes it back to us safe and sound. If you wish, you may also continue with the festivities. We must have complete faith in him."

Midians were starting to leave the Great Hall. Elle wanted to stay and wait for Mike to return, but then, it wouldn't do any good if she wasted all her time worrying. She still had to figure out how to use Eve's Sea Dweller Whilom.

Elle found herself wandering around the castle and got herself lost with all its winding passageways until she was able to find a door that led her out to a small garden. It overlooked the forest. But as the castle moved in the sky, the forest drifted like an ocean below them.

Elle curiously gazed up at the majestic castle. It was bright colored with spires. She couldn't quite describe the design, but it did look like it was something in between a cathedral and a castle. Elle took a deep breath and took it all in, the beauty and magnificence of the place.

She walked along the path that cut through a bed of flowers and sat comfortably on a marble bench. It had been a cloudy day and Elle noticed that the castle was heading right into one huge clump of cloud. Soon, the entire place became completely enveloped in fog.

Elle took out the perfectly round pearl onto her palm. *There must be a secret to using this*, she thought. First, she tried to concentrate all her energy over it. She tried to conjure up that experience she had during her test in Atlantis—when she had invoked the white light—but nothing happened.

She shook the pearl and juggled it and even made it touch different elements: the leaves, the soil, the bench—but still nothing. She sighed and clutched the pearl tightly in her palm.

The Tree of Life is going to be so disappointed in me. I've gone through so much in order to become a Sky Dweller like everyone said I would be… but, why aren't I? What could possibly be hindering me from transcending? I want to be a Sky Dweller so badly. If I could just transcend now, then maybe I could help Mike by being a part of the army. If I could just will it hard enough, then by now I would have had feathers that spanned so wide and full of prowess that I could glide with the wind under my wings.

When Elle opened her eyes, she found blue feathers coming out of her shoulder blades. *Is this really happening? Did I just transcend?* She twirled around in circles, but like a ghost, the wings slowly vanished into thin air. Oh! It must have been the pearl's doing. Maybe some sort of illusion.

Elle decided to head back inside to tell Erin about it when she heard a noise from behind the bushes.

Glowing yellow eyes sliced through the fog and her fight-or-flight-response started to kick in. As the wolf came into sight, Elle immediately noticed that it wasn't growling and its back hairs weren't prickling up. The wolf was just looking at her with a stunned expression. Before Elle could do anything, the wolf had sprinted toward her, gradually turning into man. The next thing she knew, Sunny had already sealed her lips with a passionate kiss like that of a bewildered lover.

"Daphne. Is it really you?"

Sunny's face was filled with ardor, but Elle was too dumbfounded to speak.

"Sorry? I-I'm not… and you're not using dark magic on me," Elle found herself saying. It dawned on her that it must have been the effect of the pearl. *Could it have projected the person that he had longed to see? Oh, this is NOT good!*

"I've missed you. Of course not! Why would I do such a thing?" he replied. Sunny had that same regal quality to him just like Luna, his twin sister.

"Sunny, would it be okay if I ask you to be my teacher?" Elle asked. It came a little too late to realize just how stupid it sounded.

"What is it you need to learn?"

"I-I want to learn how I could keep my Free Will. Is there a way that I could resist dark magic? I mean, what better way to learn how to resist it than the one who actually knows how it works, right?"

"I can teach you how to block mind control. I can also teach you how to use dark magic if you want."

"Oh. No! Umm… blocking is more than enough," she replied.

"Well, it's pretty easy. You see, on earth, there are these so-called hypnotists who would snap their fingers so that the one being hypnotized would snap back to reality."

"Okay?" she replied.

"So, you just have to hold on to that snap—it's that something that you go back to, to remember who you are. Mine just happens to be you."

Elle nodded slowly as she thought about her grandfather.

"Daphne," Sunny said as he held her hand. "I don't even know if you're real but I really did want to see you one last time, that's why I wanted Jon to make an image of you. I don't deserve you. I've been rash."

How long is he going to see me as a different person? Elle tried to compose herself, "It wasn't Jon's fault—you should know that. If you ever loved Daphne, then set her free."

Sunny hugged her tight and whispered in her ear. "I will try. I will try to do as you wish. Maybe I could still be the man worthy of your love, my Daphne." Then he looked at her so earnestly that she felt her own heart ache. He gently touched her cheek. "I will do everything for you. I know now what I must do." Sunny turned away and was gone through the fog in a single leap.

Elle slumped down on the grass, her heart still racing. She didn't know if she had done the right thing but it seemed to have given Sunny the closure that he needed. She touched her lips and thought of Mike.

When Elle got back inside the castle, she overheard Erin talking to one of the castle guards.

"Hey," she said. "Have you seen a silver haired girl walk around here? She's wearing a blue dress. And she would most likely look like she's lost."

The guard shook his head.

"Okay. Well. If you do, please lead her to the arena."

"Erin!" Elle called out from across the corridor.

"Elle? Where have you been? I've been looking all over for you."

"I was out on the garden. I think I know how to use the pearl now," Elle said as she came up to her. "Can you help me send a message to my mother in Atlantis? I need to tell her that Jon won't need to hide any longer. I've spoken to Sunny, and I think he's okay now."

"You what? He could've hurt you really bad. How did it happen?"

As they walked toward the arena, Elle told her about the pearl and how it made her look like Daphne. But Elle also couldn't stop worrying about Mike and thought that maybe Erin could help enlighten her.

"So, about Mike… how long do you think he's going to be in Gethsemane?" she asked.

"I'm afraid I don't know the answer to that," replied Erin.

"I can't believe he's an Archangel now," Elle said. "But why does he have to go there in the first place?"

"Mike will be seeing bits and pieces of the future from there. When he comes back, he might be different. I think there is something about knowing what the future holds that could really mess with someone's head. I can only hope that he will be able to pull himself through somehow."

Erin introduced Elle to the other Sky Dwellers when they arrived in the arena. It was a circular space outside the castle that had stone benches for a good number of people.

Elle dueled with Erin as Midians started to fill up the benches. Even Amos and his flock were there—all hooting and clapping. In a way, it seemed like Elle and Erin had become a part of the festival's main attractions.

Erin was a strong opponent. She seemed to dance like a feather in the wind, but her sword struck with great force as if she was using the wind around her for the extra boost. She did have two sets of wings, so Elle had to adjust her fighting style. After a while, she was able to see the pattern in a way that only a student who trained under the same instructor would notice. Mike had taught her well, but now, she had the edge and was able to anticipate her next move. The duel ended with the Tranquil Blade splitting Erin's sword in half. Everyone stood up with a roaring applause.

Erin came up to her and shook her hand. "That was a good fight. I think you'll do us proud, Elle."

"Thanks. I'll probably need more training though."

As Elle treaded back for the castle, there were children and stall vendors who enthusiastically called out to her and gave her all sorts offerings. They handed out trinkets and candies and stuff she didn't even know the use for, and in exchange, they begged her to protect Eden from harm. This startled Elle and all she could do was to nod in their direction.

Elle went back to her room. She took a good long bath and got in bed. But, for some reason, she kept tossing and turning. Her nerves were on the edge so she ended up going for a walk. She strolled around the castle, admiring the frescoes until she found herself in the Great Hall to wait for Mike's return.

She must have fallen asleep because when she opened her

eyes, some of the Sky Dwellers were starting to prepare the tables for breakfast. Elle quickly got up from her seat and knelt along Gethsemane. She peered into the darkness that was illuminated with constellations. Along the glassy depths, Elle saw claws scratching and trying to break the firmament from inside. It kept pounding from the other side and her heart raced along with it. Immediately, she took out the Tranquil Blade to slice one side of the firmament, but another Sky Dweller had appeared into the Great Hall and had pierced it ahead of her. Black mist began to fuse out from the perforation, filling the air with a sickening smell. A beak thrust out of it—it's nostrils breathing deep and then it struggled out. It tore the firmament wider revealing a burning red Phoenix covered in misty blackness. It made a shrieking scream before dropping beside her. Slowly the phoenix shape-shifted and there, lying on his back, was Mike. He kept shivering and his face looked like he was hurting. The Sky Dwellers inside the hall quickly ran to his aid.

Elle watched them as they brought him away. She was still taking deep breaths and feeling light-headed from the black mist. She couldn't shake off that petrified look on his face.

Mike must have seen something bad happen. *Are we going to fail the same way Adam and Eve had?* She clasped her palms to her face. She had to be strong. Somehow. But amid her anxieties, she felt relieved that Mike was back.

CHAPTER TWENTY

- Mike -

In Gethsemane, Mike saw Elle die right before his eyes.

And it continued to crush him in his dreams.

He would see her die again.

And again.

And again.

CHAPTER TWENTY-ONE

- Elle -

In bed, Mike's eyebrows furrowed like he was having a bad dream.

"Man, he looks awful," Amos said. "Do you think he'll be alright?"

Erin glanced at him and then at Mike. "Well, he should… No. He must."

Elle sat on Mike's bedside and held his hand, "Can he tell us about what happened inside Gethsemane? I really wish he would."

"No. He cannot tell anyone. Whatever the Creator revealed to him, that is his burden. His alone." Erin sighed and sank in resignation onto a nearby chair.

From the window behind Erin, Elle saw something fly toward Higher Gan.

"Finchy?" she whispered to herself. Elle stood up and went for the door. "I'll be back. I just have to go check on something," Elle said before walking out of the room and out of the castle.

Finchy was flying so fast that he almost crashed onto the pavement. "Elle! It's an emergency!" shouted the enormous finch.

Elle ran up to Finchy and helped him up. "What's going on?"

Kick, who was on his back, leaped up to her. Elle was able to catch him with cupped hands.

His thin cricket wings kept fluttering with tension. "Elle! Hurry! It's Willow. She's in danger!"

Without completely knowing the situation, Elle immediately burst into action.

"Kick, go get Amos and Erin," she ordered. "Finchy, take me to where Willow is!"

She hopped onto Finchy's back and they were soon flying away.

They flew a few miles from Higher Gan, toward a craggy mountain terrain.

"So, what exactly happened?" Elle asked as she peered into the horizon.

"You see," Finchy said. "this morning there were Sky Dwellers who passed by the house. They were the ones who told us of your whereabouts and we decided to come over and see you. While we were on our way, we took a shortcut along the highest peak of that ridge. It seemed harmless, but now I know why Midians never take that route. Because something just attacked us out of nowhere! We couldn't see it but whatever it was, it's definitely powerful."

Elle could see the peak from a distance. "Okay. But what happened to Willow? Why isn't she with you?"

"I don't know. She said she would create a diversion to help us escape and just flew away on her own. I'm really hoping that nothing bad happens to her. She's a flying squirrel, so she's small and fast. And she's good at hiding herself."

They both hushed as they approached the mountain. Finchy

flew low to the ground so they could check for signs of movement. The mountain was steep and its foliage draped with vines and thorns.

"Over there!" Elle said. From a distance, there was a glint of light that swept past the trees. It immediately caught her eye. Pretty soon, huge branches came crashing down on them. Luckily, Finchy was able to maneuver away swiftly.

"What was that? Some kind of weapon?" Elle asked before hearing a swishing sound sweep past her along with a trail of blur.

"Ouch!" Elle looked down and found her arm bleeding. "Who are you? Why are you doing this?" she shouted.

Elle took out the Tranquil Blade from its sheath and closed her eyes to listen to the whirring sound. In a split second, she opened her eyes and swung her sword. It made a loud *tink* and there was something that wobbled from the blur. Elle looked at it closely and knew exactly what she was looking at. "It's Eve's Sky Dweller Whilom!" Again it swung away out of view. "But how is that Sphere moving on its own? That's impossible! Do you think maybe I could catch it?"

"I think you're out of your mind to even think that!" cried Finchy.

"If that Sphere really belonged to Eve, then I could try to make it recognize me as its new owner," Elle said to Finchy.

"And how exactly are you going to do that?" he replied doubtfully.

Elle's grip on Finchy's feathers tightened and at the top of her lungs she cried, "Hey you! It's me Uriel, the granddaughter of Adam and Eve. Please come back, we need you!"

The Sphere whirled faster, busily slicing air molecules like it was thirsty for blood. Finchy lunged away quickly and made a loud grunt.

"Okay. Please stop asking it to come back to you. If it does, it's definitely going to split us in half!"

"Think! Think! Think!" Elle blurted out in frustration. "What do people do to catch a speeding bullet? Oh! Maybe we could get it stuck somewhere!"

"Alright. It's worth to try." Finchy flew as fast as he could and maneuvered near tree trunks but it was hopeless, the Sphere was able to cut through the thickest of them.

"Okay, that didn't work the way I thought it would. If my grandfather were here, what would he do?" That's when it dawned on her. He would sing! Yes, he would most certainly sing his heart out. She had to sing his favorite song about the the Story of the Lost Halo.

"Finchy, I need you to put me down on the ground and get away from here as far away as you can."

"What?! I'm not leaving you with that thing!"

"Trust me. Just do as I say."

Finchy glided down a clearing where Elle could dismount.

"Tell the others to stay away. Not even Erin and Amos. Now go," she said as she slid down his back and ran as fast as she could.

Finchy looked at her worriedly before flying away.

If I can't command you, then I'm going to woo you, Elle said to herself.

She tried to sing as clearly and as loudly as she could, "Hello-halo-hello! I'm happy we meet again!" Elle fumbled a little with the melody because the Sphere kept on thrashing here and there. Branches kept collapsing along her path.

"I know you've been used against your purpose. Wronged and lost in the woods of time. But the fight isn't over, no, not yet. You have to come back to me, to the one whom you belong. I will not escape you. I will not betray you. So, find me now, my loyal sphere, before it's too late."

Elle leaped away from fallen branches as she tried to remember the next line. "I've hurdled great lengths and travelled far and wide. You know I've climbed endless heights and taken leaps of faith. Yes, you know it. It's always been me. It's time you remember me!"

At that moment, the Sphere sliced toward her. It had missed her waist, but not her dress. Her flashlight keychain flew from the ripped pocket. *No!* It was the last gift her grandfather gave. Elle launched herself to catch it, but it was on its away toward a cliff. She continued to extend her arm and the next thing she knew, her feet were completely over the edge.

Elle was able to catch it but it was going to be a long way down. It was her training with Mike that helped her remain calm and collected in situations like this, giving her the presence of mind that she needed to successfully cling onto the side of the precipice.

She quickly slipped the keychain inside her belt bag and climbed her way up, but alas, one of the rocks that she held onto broke off and she started to fall straight down. One last time Elle heard the Sphere careen towards her and then she felt a strong pulse sweep across the forest.

PART V:
RAPTURE

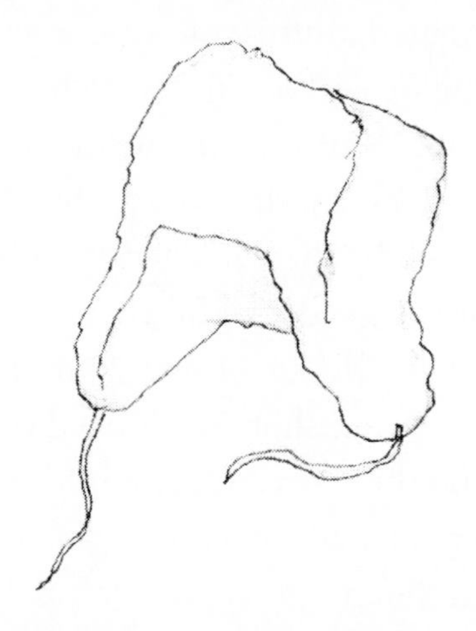

CHAPTER TWENTY-TWO

- Elle -

The cold was making Elle's face and fingers numb. Her eyes opened slightly as she tried to regain consciousness. She struggled to sit up and continued to shiver as she started to inspect herself. No injuries. Just a few minor scrapes and a nagging headache smack on her temple.

Elle breathed warmth onto her cupped hands and looked at her surroundings. She must have fallen onto a body of water and got swept onto the riverbank. For a moment everything was frozen still, like the cold had stopped time itself. Even the dust in the atmosphere seemed petrified, but it didn't frighten her. What got her heart racing was finding herself embraced in darkness. She was no longer in Eden.

The full moon hung in the clear sky above her, casting a long streak of light along the forest where the first flurries of snow glistened as it fell.

From a distance, Elle heard a loud thud coming from behind the trees. Quickly gathering her wits, she stood up.

"Elle? Elle!" shouted a little voice. Between the trees, a small shape came sprinting up and down toward her.

"Pim, is that you? Why are you outside of Eden?" Elle asked, but before she could say another word, Pim had already leaped into her arms, followed by the wretched sound of a rifle going off. Elle pulled Pim close as she ducked with her belly on the ground.

What is that? Elle felt something cold and solid tug at her elbow. She must have been shot. She looked down at it. Near her elbow, half-buried on the shore, was the Sphere. She motioned her hand to reach for it but it had somehow dislodged itself to meet her hand. *Ouch!* She muttered out under her breath. "Try being a bit gentler next time," she said with a start.

She saw the same dragon mark engraved on the Sphere. Finally, she has three of Eve's Whiloms. All she needed was—

Bang!

A second gunshot echoed even louder through the forest. Without a second thought, Elle carried Pim and started running toward the other side of the woods.

"Pim, please don't tell me you travelled by moon alone?"

"Uhmm, I can't do that yet. It's really all because of Momma. She ordered me to clean the house, but I didn't want to. That's why I snuck onto Luna's moon ray. Oh, she'll get really mad at me. I beg you, please don't tell her!"

"Oh Pim, you didn't… Where's Luna now?"

"I don't know. She—"

"Shhhh! Someone's coming."

Elle pushed Pim up onto the branch of a tree. She was about to climb up when she heard a soft rustle from the bushes. She had no choice but to wish that the Sphere would obey her.

She placed the Sphere over her head. At first it felt like she was drowning. She clutched at her neck and tried to gasp for air.

It was too much. She would have to remove the Sphere off of her head. If not, then she might just die of asphyxiation. Elle raised her hand toward her head, but upon looking closely, she saw that her arms were becoming translucent. She must have vanished without her realizing it. Everything around her was shifting and turning like half of her body was elsewhere in some other dimension. Everything in front of her turned into smudges of shapes of white and grey. It felt so unreal that it scared her, as if she was in someone else's bad dream, like a combination of vertigo and drowsy pills. She stood closer to the tree and held her breath trying to calm herself. It somehow did the trick. Things were starting to look clearer as she tried to focus.

From the corner of her eyes, she saw a brawny man appear. He had a snarl on his face and was wearing a checkered shirt and a cap with earflaps. He was definitely a hunter. Elle had no way of knowing if he was a good person or not or if he would let a fourteen-year-old girl go because she was human. It just didn't feel right to trust a stranger with a rifle pressed close to his chest, ready to go off at any moment. He walked straight toward her and sniffed the air.

Elle tried hard not to breathe, but just then, a smile traced the side of his face.

The hunter had moved to the back of the tree. *Oh No! He must have sniffed out Pim.* Immediately, Elle grabbed the Sphere off of her head and threw it toward the other side of the forest. The Sphere came thrashing at the bushes and distracted the hunter, making him run towards the sound.

Elle took Pim out of the tree and carried him down.

"Finally, we're safe!" Pim exclaimed as he looked over Elle's shoulder.

"What?"

Elle turned around to look behind her.

Nearby, a luminous beam of light was glowing downward. They could see Luna, her face angry amid her graceful descent.

"Pim, you're in for a lot of trouble, young man, and—what is this? Elle? What are you doing here?"

"Luna… I, I'm sorry," Pim apologized.

"Please don't do that again, Pim. Now come, both of you."

Pim took a few steps further when his foot stepped on the hunter's cap. He looked conspiratorially at Elle before ducking towards it and putting it on. It sat half-tilting on his head. It was a memento, but somehow Pim managed to wear the cap like it was his to begin with.

They both walked over to Luna as she shape-shifted into a deer and motioned her head like she was urging them to ride her. Elle picked up Pim, and they mounted the deer's back.

Luna started to run in a circle along the beam of light until they began to float. Meanwhile, a whirring sound alerted Elle. She reached her hand out to meet it. This time, the sphere tried to slow down as it approached her palm.

"Easy does it. That's better. We'll need to learn to work together from now on, okay?" she said as she clasped her hand around it and tucked it onto a carabiner under her belt.

They started to float higher and higher. From above the trees, Elle could see the hunter running and screaming his head off. Close behind him was a lion, but unlike any lion she had ever seen. This one had pristine white fur. The hunter was fumbling to reload his rifle that he stumbled and dropped his gun. He wouldn't be able to reach it in time. The lion was already too near so there was no other choice but to continue to run. Once out of view, the white lion remained prowling along the gun and slowly shape-shifted into a man.

"Dad?" Elle couldn't believe her eyes. Her dad grabbed the gun and with brute force he broke the rifle in half.

Luna leaned her head towards Elle. "Don't worry, your father's a lion. He knows how to deal with hunters." She said as she continued to gallop through the thick clouds that smeared the night sky.

"Luna, I won't be going back to Eden," she said. "If possible, could you take me home?"

"Your home… here? Why would you want to stay here?" Luna asked in surprise.

"The last one is Eve's Wanderer's Whilom. If I am to find it, then it would most definitely be outside of Eden because there are no Wanderers in Eden. I'll be fine. Don't worry."

§

Elle said goodbye to Pim and Luna as they dropped her off in front of her house.

"Thank you, Luna," she said before breaking in through the front door. Once inside, Elle started searching for clues of the location of the last Whilom, but it was useless. She kept looking for possible hiding places—inside drawers, under the tables, the rug, the chandelier—until she noticed that morning had caught up with her.

"Hello? Is anybody there?" Elle froze when she heard the front door creak open. "If there is, you shouldn't be here, breaking into houses is against the law."

At the front door, Paige's face appeared.

"You've got to be kidding me!" Paige cried out, surprised. She had dropped the gardening shears she was holding up.

"You crazy girl!" she said as ran and hugged her. "Elle! I've missed you and I've been worried sick! Are you aware that you've been gone for half a school year? And what in the world are you wearing?"

"Paige! I've missed you too," Elle replied. "Sorry I wasn't able to let you know how I was. It's a long story, believe me."

Elle stepped on top of a stool and reached upward to open a compartment in the ceiling.

"It's so weird. I've tried to track you down only to find you at your place! What gives? I saw the front door cracked open. And by the way, did you see your parents already? I heard they moved out of town since you went missing. And just what are you looking for inside that filthy thing?"

"I'm looking for something. Paige, you know I trust you right? It's about my family. I guess. We're not so different after all. I just found out that my family had secrets too. Well, I could tell you everything, but I need you to promise me that—"

Elle was cut short when Paige impatiently dragged her down from the stool. "Could you please stop what you're doing? You're coming with me. Tell me all about it in the car. I still need to get the groceries done. I think we'll also need to fix you up so you could join my family for Christmas dinner. I mean really, you look awful. If they ever find you wearing that, I'm going to have to tell them that you've been cosplaying."

Elle gave a broad smile. "Food sounds good right about now."

Out of the front door, Paige and Elle darted for the red pickup.

Once in the driver's seat, Paige realized that she had left the keys in the ignition. *Just great.*

"Don't tell my mom I left the keys and the door unlocked when I left the car. Actually, no. Don't tell her about the car. We were never here," she said.

Elle sat on the passenger seat and nervously latched her

seatbelt tight.

"Okay, now spill!" Paige said as she drove the car off the side street.

"Okay," Elle said, "just make sure you drive safely, and take it easy on the gas. And before I tell you anything, you should maybe forget everything we studied in the library about genetics. What I'm about to tell you is borderline odd."

§

Paige's grim and candy-colored room was very much like her—an array of contradictions. Like a gothic unicorn had farted poisonous posies in it. There were skulls and flowers and the most colorful stuff against black walls. Elle stretched out on the bed after having a good long shower. Paige lent her some of her clothes, and as she tidied up her things, she checked inside her pocket for the keychain.

"Thanks for dinner, Paige. Your family has always been so nice."

"Really? I thought dinner went horribly. I'm sorry my folks kept asking questions about your disappearance and all. And my uncle was just way too weird."

"So, how about it? You must think I'm just as crazy like your uncle. I mean, with everything I've told you."

"Hmmm, kind of... but not today. Today, I'm just happy my friend is back. Besides, at least now I can take my revenge on you after all the worry you've caused me," Paige said as she hit Elle in the arm with a stuffed teddy bear.

Elle instinctively counter attacked with a pillow. The rumble was definitely on. Soon, they were both throwing pillows and stuffed toys at each other as they ran around and giggled, filling the room with floating cotton and feathers. They were jumping on the bed so much that Elle's keychain fell onto the floor. Their laughter died the moment they heard a cracking sound. It was Paige, accidentally stepping on the keychain that Adam had given Elle.

"Omigosh! I'm so sorry! I didn't mean to!" Paige exclaimed.

Elle reached down to pick it up, but there was something inside that came out from the crack and rolled out onto the floor. It was something round and tiny.

"What is that?" Elle said, more curious than upset.

Paige tilted her head. She picked it up and looked at it closely. "I think it's a seed."

"Why would there be a seed inside my keychain? Unless—" Elle's eyes widened. "Paige, would you happen to have a magnifying glass?"

Elle checked the seed from under a magnifying glass and saw the exact same markings on it, like it was purposefully etched with a dragon's head design. "It's definitely the last Whilom. I can't believe it! I had been carrying it all this time!"

"Could it be?" Paige said. "The seed from the forbidden fruit? The one that Eve took a bite out of?"

"I really wouldn't know. I haven't finished reading my grandfather's journal," replied Elle.

"Now that you have all four, what exactly do you do with them?" Paige asked. Elle laid all the items onto the bed: the Seed, the Sphere, the Pearl, and the Sword. "I think I should go back to Eden and ask the Tree of Life. I'm sure she'll know what to do next."

That night, even though she was exhausted, Elle still couldn't sleep. She couldn't help but think about Mike.

When morning came, Elle quickly got up from bed even though her muscles ached. Some of the bruises and scrapes on her arms and legs were still visible.

At the breakfast table, Elle and Paige tried to act normal, but when it was finally just the two of them, they couldn't help but talk about how they were going to get inside Eden.

"You see in Eden, some trees are guarded by fairies," Elle said. "And since fairies are Sky Dwellers, too, then there's a big chance they could help us. I think I know a tree here on earth where a fairy might live—one powerful enough to get us there and powerful enough to protect the oldest tree in the world."

"Why, of course," Paige replied with a smirk on her face, "How could I ever forget the tree that got us both in trouble in the first place?"

Elle had to laugh. "I know, right? Anyway, the plan is to meet that fairy."

Paige looked anxious and worried, but then again, she was still probably trying to accept her as her new crazy friend.

They loaded their backpacks with provisions and stormed out of the house after the Christmas morning merriment had died down. The bus ride took ages, but Elle felt hopeful. Her plan might actually work.

When they arrived, they set out on a trek down a dirt path. The sun was blazing on their foreheads.

After some time, Elle finally stopped walking. "We're here!"

They both sat on the foot of the tree. Elle tilted her head upwards and checked the branches above them as they both drank water from their tin cans.

"Okay. So what now?" asked Paige as she wiped away the sweat off her forehead.

"From here," Elle said, "I think we should be able to summon the fairy even without the enchantment."

Before she could say another word, a gust of wind blew, and the dust whirred around the tree from the bottom up.

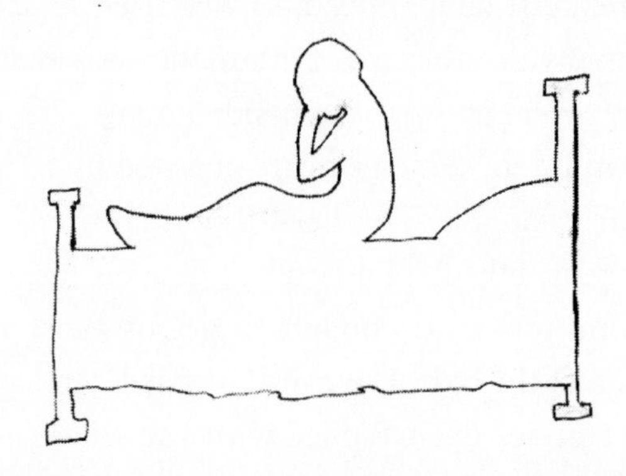

CHAPTER TWENTY-THREE

- Mike -

Mike could hear people talking around him but he couldn't seem to wake up.

"Aeris," he heard Amos say. "Have you located Elle?"

There was a pause before he said, "Really? You have?"

Mike could feel Aeris' tiny hands as she tried to pull his eyelids open.

All of a sudden, Mike stopped shivering, and he heard a different voice. He couldn't make out what it was saying, but after hearing it, Mike was able to open his eyes. In front of him, he could see Aeris about to smack his nose with a twig.

"Mike! Finally! We need to go now!" shouted Amos.

CHAPTER TWENTY-FOUR

- Elle -

A fairy with crescent moon spectacles appeared from between the barks of the tree. She was old and frail-looking. She peeked out and immediately smiled after seeing Elle.

"Oh! What a wonderful surprise!"

"Y-you remember me?"

"Why, of course I do. I never forget a face," she said, but the moment the fairy stepped out of the tree, a snake had appeared. It sprang up and coiled its body around her, squeezing her tight.

"No! Stop! Leave her alone!" shouted Elle.

"Well then," the snake said, "looks like somebody wants to be a hero. How about a bargain?"

"What kind of bargain?" Elle asked.

"I want you to give me the Whiloms. Then, I'll take you with me as my ransom, my new Eve. If you agree, I will let her go."

The fairy shook her head. "No, dear. Just let it be. You still have your life ahead of you. I am ready for it. I always knew this day would come."

"No," Elle said. "I won't let it happen. He doesn't scare me, not anymore. If I was meant for something great, then it starts with me doing something good, just like my grandfather."

"So, is that a yes?" asked the Serpent as he slithered from a branch.

"Yes," replied Elle.

At that moment, Mike and twelve other Sky Dwellers had come down from between the clouds.

The Serpent kept hissing as he summoned other Wanderers to his aid. The ground began to rumble. The land started to crack and erupt with steam. From the opening, all sorts of reptiles came out and fought with the Sky Dwellers. Elle couldn't believe her eyes. It was like she had seen all this before. Like it was a scene that had come out from her nightmare. Reptiles eating feathered creatures, but in this case, in the form of Midians. She saw Mike, Erin and Amos fight against gorgons and other monstrous beings.

The Serpent too started to transform into a huge monster with an assortment of reptile-like body parts. It's claws immediately grabbed hold of Elle as it threw the fairy to the ground. Breaking free from it's clutches was impossible and the next thing she knew, she was being dragged into one of the cracks on the ground from where the reptiles had come.

§

The demon dropped Elle onto the floor of a soot-stained lair. He grabbed her sword, necklace, Sphere, and the Seed from her belt bag, and placed them in one corner.

"That boy can't save you now. Seriously, why do you fight me?

Demons exist for a reason. My dear, you should know, this world is filled with deception."

He then started walking around in circles. "The Creator's ways, well, they're—how shall I say it? Unpredictable. You see, even when you are under the care of the light, you will always cast a shadow. It always is, the nearer you get to that light, the larger your shadow becomes."

"You mean you've been close to the light?" Elle asked. "Are you the reason why the Creator forbade everyone to eat the fruit from the Tree? If so, that means you are—"

The demon cut her off, saying, "Yes. You finally get it. My name… is Eden."

Fire blazed in Eden's eyes. The rage in his voice bore a thousand years of hatred.

"It is in my house that you dwell, in my garden that creatures frolic. It was I who brought it to its most glorious state! I was alone. I was so powerful that nothing could possibly get in my way. I remember a time when I did good things and people would worship me and mock me and hate me. Free Will gave me the means to be selfish and playful. I no longer fear Him now, child."

"But at what cost?" Elle asked.

"Oh, such hypocrisy. Evil comes in different forms, my dear. There is darkness in everyone, the animals, the Midians, even Sky Dwellers. Darkness gets to us when we least expect it, but it will come."

"But what about second chances?" Elle asked.

"What about them? How many had to die in that great flood? How many had to die during those times that He Himself cleansed the world? I care about humanity more than He does! I give man what their heart desires while the Creator makes his greatest followers suffer for his cause. I am the balance. I am both Good and Evil! You see, He is afraid of me. He once asked me to rejoin Him. Ha! Rejoin Him? If I did, then what happens to me? Why would I want to lose myself? To become a mere concept? A faceless coward who doesn't face those he loves? Why do you want us to be our truest selves just to give it all up in the end? And He couldn't answer me. I, I who have loved Him all my life."

Elle paused. Inside her was a quiet revelation. There were three pillars in Eden, one for each race. Eden must have been the fourth. The one who led the race of Wanderers.

"I think it's you who loved Him more than anyone," she said. "I haven't really spoken with Him the same way you have back in Eden. Maybe I don't even know Him well enough to say that I love Him well enough. You've simply buried Him with rage deep inside of you—but He should still be there. I saw the Creator in him, my grandfather. Contrary to what you say, the Creator does face those He loves, because He is us. We are Him."

At that moment, Eden glowed.

"No! He is not! Shut up!" the serpent cried furiously in torment.

It could have been his imagination or the work of the Pearl, but it was as if Eden was beginning to see the Creator in Elle's face. He fell to his knees as he battled with himself. "I—I'm—"

"Tell me, Eden. Who is your greatest enemy?" Elle asked. "Is it not that our greatest enemy has always been ourselves? The only thing that could ever stop you from being your truest self is you. Free Will is a gift. If taken away, then you will merely be a machine. Can't you see? We all have the capacity for change. Who you are is an outcome of Free Will. If Free Will can destroy you, then Free Will can also save you."

Eden roared even louder in anger and agony. The den shook as fire blew out with a loud bang. He threw her body against a wall.

The pain was excruciating. Elle tried to concentrate and managed to look straight at Eden.

"*He who loves truly never loses entirely.* He never yearned to defeat you, Eden. You were never forsaken."

Just then, Elle began to float and was suspended in midair. She closed her eyes and focused her energy to summon the white light. *This is how I die.* Everything she had, she offered it to Eden.

She was moments away from her final breath, and she whispered her last words, "Genuine kindness requires strength. Genuine kindness requires love. Genuine kindness requires sacrifice."

Eve's four Whiloms glowed as her aura left her body, its energy powerful enough to open a rift as Elle gave every last bit of herself into the opening, until she saw her life flash before her eyes.

Eden's eyes widened. His heart felt a familiar ache. In the blaze, Eden saw through the freshly opened portal, his garden, his house, and the vast lands that were filled with wondrous and beautiful creatures. Through her was the portal to the Garden of Eden. Through her, Eden felt the warmth, the love, and the life that flowed inside it. He remembered the moments when he wandered freely over the hills, when he planted seedlings, a time when he used his hands to build and create. He was reminded of life's simplicity and the joy it brought him. It was then that all became clear to him. He closed his eyes. A demon in his most silent prayer.

Eden reached out and touched her shoulder.

"Uriel, please stop… that is enough. Forgive me. Please forgive me." Eden's eyes widened. "I guess this is checkmate. The Pawn has reached the end of the board. Farewell to you, dear queen, and thank you."

Eden lifted his head up. "The Creator had sacrificed His son to open up His kingdom for mankind. I guess, this is the time I sacrifice myself to open up Eden, the Eden I've fought hard to reclaim has always been mine to give."

A tear fell as Eden opened his palms, and he looked at them with reverence.

"I see Him in you, and I am so angry. You made me love you, and you allowed me to hate you." He dug his hands into the earth and recited the words. "I... Eden... open the gates of my most beloved land, for all to embrace who they are, for all to continue living their life by the greatest design there is, and for all to have a chance to transcend and be their truest selves."

Everything went white, and the Earth's gates connected itself to Eden, a world where the Creator's love flowed endlessly. Eden smiled and was no more.

In the deep recesses of man's soul, the Sky Dwellers woke from their slumber. Countless men and women from different nations floated weightlessly above the ground: people in fields, shops, in offices, and on the streets. They levitated and heard the call from inside of them.

Before Elle closed her eyes, she saw a flash of red charging in from the portal, reaching out for her.

CHAPTER TWENTY-FIVE

- Mike -

As the white light covered the land, Mike was able to push through the portal from inside Eden—grabbing Elle from the den that was engulfed in flames. She was in his arms now.

"His promise has been fulfilled Elle. It is done."

Mike took her through the portal. Once on the other side, he rushed her to the Tree of Life, but Elle was already slipping away.

The moment they reached the Tree, Mike plucked a handful of leaves.

"Forgive me," he said. "I just need some healing."

Mike dropped to his knees and laid the leaves onto her body. Nothing happened. Softly, the massive tree called back to him and asked.

"Mike, shall I take her now?"

"No. She can't die. No." Mike got up and reached out his hand once more—this time toward a fruit.

There was a pause before the Tree of Life said, "I know what you're thinking, Michael. You know it's forbidden."

"But why? What's the cost of taking one fruit compared to saving a life?"

Mike felt it calling to him. "This fruit, it's the only thing that could save her. I'm not going to let her die like this." He held it in his hand and was in deep thought. "Could it bring her back?" But the tree did not answer. Then he whispered, "Of course it could."

Once more, he took a good look at Elle. "It's my decision. Whatever the cost, I'll take it."

His hand was on the fruit as he pulled it closer, but before it was plucked, Mike stopped. It just occured to him after noticing one little detail that he had missed. How was Elle unscathed from the fiery den? Maybe it wasn't the Demon that had killed her. Did she willingly sacrifice herself? He couldn't find any burn marks.

Mike's eyes widened. He felt his body shake uncontrollably as it dawned on him. Mike kissed her forehead and held her tightly in his arms. "I'm so sorry," he whispered, "I've been so blind." Hot tears continued to fall down his face.

Flames began coursing through his body as he turned into a phoenix.

Mike took her up past the clouds and higher as the daylight crept along the floating stars and into the darkest, most unknown part of the sky. Then he began flying in a circular path faster than he had ever flown. He created a red blaze that enveloped them both into a ball of fire. The flames grew larger and larger and the heat rose higher until he couldn't see, hear, or feel anymore. That's when the blaze began transforming, changing in color. From inside crawled a tiny spark of blue that furiously devoured and spread itself outward, covering them.

A blue flame. Warmer. Fiercer. Stronger. Why had he realized it too late? All that time he had watched over her—how could he have not noticed? He knew the reason why Elle couldn't transcend. It was because *he* was still alive. It was because of *him*. The world had space for only one phoenix. He had no other half whatsoever, or so he thought.

There was no telling what would happen now. It was going to be him or her—or someone else entirely.

EXCERPT FROM BOOK 2

The flames started dying
Flickering no more
The death of both Sky Dwellers
Now merged to the core

From the ashes
A child was born
A blue phoenix
Stronger than ever before

ACKNOWLEDGMENTS

It took me three years to write this book and I'm so relieved now that I've given birth to this first novel. I thank our Creator for giving me the strength and the will to pursue this journey. I'm also grateful for having such a loving and supportive family. I know that my grandfather would have been very proud.

To my Igniting Souls family, and Kary Oberbrunner, thank you. Your encouragement and insight have been invaluable. Also, a shower of thanks to Chris, Gio, Steve LeBel, and Myrna Fay Flick for all the help and inspiration. I still owe you guys coffee.

I would also like to give a shoutout to Mina V. Esguerra for providing such amazing tips. To my editors Chersti Nieveen, Marie Mones, and Marjorie Kramer, you're all amazing. To the people who spared their time to read my work: Cel, XY, Carl, Jio, Mark and RJ, your feedbacks were greatly appreciated. Thanks also to my professors, classmates, and friends.

BOOK CLUB DISCUSSION GUIDE:

1. Did the first chapter succeed in getting you hooked into the book?
2. Is the story plot-based or character driven?
3. What was the most memorable quote/passage?
4. Which location in Eden did you like the most? Why?
5. Did you find universal truths from the book?
6. Did Mike and Elle succeeded in their goal? Was it a happy ending or a sad ending?
7. Was the narration able to transport you into the world of fantasy?
8. Were you able to see change in the characters throughout the story? Did your opinion of them change?
9. How did the structure of the book (POV, timeline, syntax, choice of tense) affect the story?
10. Which characters was the most relatable? Why?
11. What are your thoughts about the ending? What are the things that you like or dislike? Was there anything you wish had been different?
12. Were there moments of realization that changed your opinion or perspective about certain things? Do you feel different after you've read the book?
13. If the book were to have a movie adaptation, who would you love to see play certain characters?

Can't get enough of The Sky Dweller series? Check out *https://ariaveil.com/* and find out which type of Midian you are: Sky Dweller, Land Dweller, Sea Dweller, or Wanderer. Remember to subscribe to our newsletter for occasional updates, exclusive promos.

ABOUT THE AUTHOR

Aria Veil is a writer and artist. She has a lot of pent-up creativity which fuels her desire to write and paint. Aria hopes that through her talents, she would be able to reach out and help others. On days when she isn't writing, Aria spends her time either thinking up new adventures or going on adventures of her own. She loves climbing mountains, riding her bike and having long walks on the beaches of her homeland, the Philippines.